Henry Robert Plomer

Robert Wyer, Printer and Bookseller

A Paper read before the Bibliographical Society, January 21st, 1895

Henry Robert Plomer

Robert Wyer, Printer and Bookseller
A Paper read before the Bibliographical Society, January 21st, 1895

ISBN/EAN: 9783337250645

Printed in Europe, USA, Canada, Australia, Japan

Cover: Foto ©Raphael Reischuk / pixelio.de

More available books at **www.hansebooks.com**

ROBERT WYER,

PRINTER AND BOOKSELLER.

ROBERT WYER,

PRINTER AND BOOKSELLER.

A PAPER
READ BEFORE THE BIBLIOGRAPHICAL SOCIETY,
JANUARY 21ST, 1895.

BY

HENRY R. PLOMER.

LONDON:
PRINTED FOR THE BIBLIOGRAPHICAL SOCIETY,
BY BLADES, EAST & BLADES,
NOVEMBER, 1897.

CONTENTS.

ROBERT WYER,
PRINTER AND BOOKSELLER.

By HENRY R. PLOMER.

Read January 21st, 1895.

OBERT WYER carried on the business of a printer and bookseller, at the sign of "St. John the Evangelist, at Charing Cross," in premises that formed part of the rentals of Norwich House, and were probably not far from where Villiers Street is now situated.

Amongst the books printed by Pynson was an edition of the popular tract of *Solomon & Marcolphus*, for sale at this house. As Pynson's death took place in 1529, Wyer was probably established there at that time, but his biography is wrapped in the greatest obscurity.

Some Wyers, members undoubtedly of this family, are found at Wendover in Bucks.[*] John Wyer, who died in 1552, held a house called the Maidenhead and half an acre of land there, but his will makes no mention of Robert. Edward Wyer of Wendover, grandson of this John, bought the *Three Cranes in the Vintry*, of Richard Tottel, as we learn from certain proceedings in Chancery.[†] But of Robert we hear nothing. Nor is there anything certain known of Robert Wyer's early career as a printer. Herbert made a note in his memorandum books that Wyer was servant to Richard Fawkes, who lived in Durham rents, close by Durham House in the Strand (*see* Dibdin, vol. iii, p. 356); in another place,[‡] the same author

---

[*] Pat. Roll. 33 H. 8, 7th part.   [†] Chancery Proceedings, 21st Eliz., No. 49.
[‡] Herbert, vol. i, p. 368.

suggests that he was apprentice to John Butler, a printer, found with the sign of "St. John the Evangelist in Fleet Street, in St. Bride's Churchyard, over against the Conduit." It has been suggested* that the two houses were one and the same; but the idea is hardly feasible. In the first place, the two localities were sufficiently wide apart to make it unlikely that any confusion could have arisen between them. The one was at the extreme east end of Fleet Street, at the bottom of Shoe Lane; the other at the extreme west end of the Strand. Besides, the men who lived in them were surely capable of describing accurately the position of their respective houses, and Wyer is as minute as Butler in many of his colophons, which declare that he lived "in St. Martin's Parish, beside Charing Crosse," and frequently give more precise particulars, as "in the Bishoppe of Norwytches Rentes." No doubt, Wyer had an interest in the Fleet Street premises. It was, I believe, this house in which John Wyer printed for some time about the year 1550, and I have no doubt in my own mind that it was this same house to which Thos. Colwell, Robert Wyer's successor, removed in the year 1565; but precisely how he came by it is not clear.

To return from conjecture to history. In the year 1536, the Bishop of Norwich's town house, of which Wyer's premises formed part of the rentals, was surrendered to King Henry VIII in exchange for certain lands in Norfolk, and a few months afterwards the King gave it to Charles Brandon, the Duke of Suffolk, who held it until his death in 1545. This transfer marks a period in the printing of Robert Wyer. Until then, he had lived in "the Bishop of Norwich's rents." Henceforward the great house close by was known as "the Duke of Suffolk's Place," and Wyer's colophons notify the change by substituting this address, a custom which he kept up long after the house had ceased to belong to any Duke of Suffolk.

In the locality successively known by these two names, we can trace Wyer at work from the year 1530 to 1556. In that year he was succeeded by a namesake, Nicholas Wyer, who printed from the same address, and in

* Mr. E. Gordon Duff made this suggestion when I read my paper on Robert Wyer, before the Library Association.

1560 by Thos. Colwell, one of William Powell's apprentices, who subsequently removed to Fleet Street, and was there in turn succeeded by Hugh
Jackson.

I have been able to make a list of nearly one hundred books printed
by Robert Wyer. Copies of no less than fifty of these are in the British
Museum; the Bodleian contains four or five not to be found elsewhere,
while the University Library at Cambridge, and the Lambeth Library have
valuable specimens of this printer's work. The remainder are described
from Herbert and Dibdin's editions of Ames' *Typographical Antiquities.* I
have not the least doubt that there are many more books of this printer's
still in existence, and that year by year fresh accessions will be made to the
list. But, as it stands, it affords a fair basis for judging his work.

The main difficulty that confronts us, in the study of Robert Wyer, is
his undated books. Out of the one hundred above mentioned, only eleven
bear any sort of date, and not all of these are dates of printing; while out
of this small number, only five or six are within the student's reach, so
that the work of attempting to classify the undated books by reference to
the dated copies, or by any method at all, is no light task.

In attempting it, I have followed as carefully as possible the methods so
successfully adopted by the late William Blades in his study of the works of
Caxton. But at the outset I found that the application of those methods
to Robert Wyer's productions was by no means so easy as from a careful
perusal of the *Life of Caxton* I was led to expect. It is difficult, indeed, for
anyone to follow clearly in Mr. Blades' footsteps who labours under the dis-
advantage of not being either a printer or typefounder by trade. The
distinction between different founts of the same type, between types re-cast
or cut down, are so minute that only a practical printer can tell the difference,
and I must confess that to this hour the mysteries of "spacing" have
baffled all my attempts to apply them to the books of Robert Wyer.
Nevertheless, I think I have achieved something, enough, I hope, at least
to form a basis for future work.

To begin with, we may at once divide the books that were printed by Robert Wyer into three broad classes.

1. Those books having the "Norwich" colophon, all of which were manifestly printed before 1537.

2. Those having the "Suffolk" colophon, which were printed after 1536.

3. Those printed for other printers, or which having only a vague colophon, stating that they were "printed by me Robert Wyer," cannot be apportioned among the two preceding classes.

Of the dated books coming into the first class (leaving out of account the *Expositiones Terminorum* mentioned by Herbert, which may have been the work of either Butler or Wyer), the British Museum has three :—*The Golden Pystle* of Richard Whytford, printed in 1531 ; Garrard's *Interpretation of the Mass* in 1532 ; and William Marshall's translation of *The Defence of Peace*, printed in 1535.

The *Golden Pystle* is printed in octavo, in the type called "Secretary," from its resemblance to the manuscript writing of the time, with Black Letter used for the first few lines of the title page and colophon. There are twenty-eight lines to a full page of the text, the type is clear, and the lower-case *w* is a larger letter, with a loop or tail carried across the top, while the lower-case *v* and *d* have a similar tail, and strokes are used for punctuation. The colophon is set up in type, and the printer's name is spelt "W Y R E," instead of "W Y E R."

The second of these three books, *The Interpretation of the Mass* (also an octavo) is identical in the character of the type and the number of lines to page with the above, but differs in this respect, that the printer's name is spelt "W Y E R" in the colophon.

The third book, the *Defence of Peace*, has not the "Norwich" colophon, though it was printed before the transfer of the house. It is a folio, and the best specimen of Robert Wyer's work that is to be found, probably the best he ever turned out. It is printed on fine paper with wide margins; the type is "Secretary," with Black Letter for the title, colophon, and headings of paragraphs. But in this work, the lower-case *w*, *v*, and *d* of the "Secretary" type are shorn of the loops seen in the two preceding books.

It is interesting to note that in one of the recently published volumes of the *State Papers of Henry the Eighth* (vol. ii, pp. 325, etc.), are letters written by the translator of this book, William Marshall, to Thomas Cromwell, from which we learn that it cost the sum of £34 to print. This would, I suppose, be equal to about £300 of our present money.

These three books then, all printed before 1536, were each of them printed in "Secretary" type, and Herbert tells us that the copy of the *Book of Hours*, which he says had an almanac dated 1533, was also printed in "Secretary."

Now, taking up the undated books with the "Norwich" colophon, I find, with only one exception, exactly the same character of type prevailing in them. The earliest of these is probably the *First Dyaloge in Englysshe*, a book of law translated from a Latin work of still earlier date. Peter Treveris printed the *Second Dialogue in English*, in the earlier part of 1531, so that Wyer may have printed his in 1530 or thereabouts. It was printed in octavo, the text in "Secretary," twenty-seven lines to the page, but with running titles, foliation, quotations, etc., in Black Letter. In the text the large lower-case *w* and *v* are seen, strokes are used in place of commas, and in addition to the printer's full page device there is a woodcut of the Royal Arms, supported by a greyhound and griffin.

The *Diurnal for Devout Souls* is identical in size and type with the foregoing, while the earlier of the two editions of the *Compost of Ptolomeus* has not only the "Norwich" colophon and all the peculiarities of setting noticed in the *Golden Pystle*, printed in 1531, but as in that book the printer's name is spelt "W Y R E" and not "W Y E R," in his device. We may therefore conclude that the date of printing must be about 1531.

In the same way many other undated books can be placed in this period, notably the *Medled Life* by William Hylton, the earlier editions of the *Antidotharius* and the *Prognostication of Erra Pater.*

In contrast with these books in "Secretary" type we have in Erasmus's *Exhortation to the Study of the Scriptures*, an octavo, with the "Norwich" colophon, but printed throughout in Black Letter, twenty-one lines to the page.

This book is by far the best specimen of Wyer's Black Letter printing that I have seen. I should imagine that the type was quite new, as the edges of the letters are sharp, every letter appears perfect, and the ink is as black as the day it was printed. No other octavo book of Wyer's printed in Black Letter that I have ever seen has twenty-one lines to the page. Altogether, I cannot fix any date for the printing of this book, but unless others turn up, to join company with it, I do not think it weakens the probability that the bulk of the books of this period were printed in "Secretary."

When we turn to the second class—the books with the "Suffolk" colophon—we find that these cover a very wide space of time, from the year 1536 down to the very year in which we lose sight of Robert Wyer altogether, the year 1556, and yet there is not a single dated book bearing this colophon. But there are books with dates subsequent to 1536, notably the *Questionary of Cyrurgeons*, printed for Richard Banckes and Henry Dabb in 1542, and several others, the date of which can be fixed by internal evidence, and all these serve as finger-posts to lead the investigator.

There is the *Assize of Bread*, a quarto, in which mention is made of a statute that was to take effect from the Feast of the Purification, in the year, "a thousande, five hundred, forty and three"; there is the *Ordinal or Statute concerning artificers*, printed for Richard Bankes, a statute enacted in 1543; more important still, there is the *Civil Nosgay*, by John Goodale, in which there are allusions to public events; "the capture of Boulogne, and the overthrow of the Scots," the latter taking place in 1547, and so giving us at least 1548 as the date of its printing, if not later. Then there is William Salisbury's *Description of the World*, with an author's preface dated 1550, and last of all, a *Prognostication*, with an Almanac for 1556.

I have made a close study of all these books, have compared one with another, and the results I have arrived at are as follows :—

The "Secretary" type continued in use for the text of all books printed down to 1542, but they have only twenty-seven lines to the full octavo page, and ordinary punctuation is used, and I would suggest that it was the old type recast. But in 1542, and from that time onwards, the order was reversed, the text of all books being printed in Black Letter, and the supplementary matter in "Secretary."

This is the arrangement found in the *Questionary of Cyrurgeons*, and other quartos, but I have based my tests mainly on the octavo books, they being by far the most numerous ; and these group themselves into two periods. Those printed between 1542 and 1550 are uniform in size, measuring in every case, after due allowance for binders' shears, $5\frac{1}{4} \times 3\frac{1}{2}$. They have twenty-four lines to the page without running titles or pagination, and rarely have the printer's device. The later books, from 1550 to 1556, have only twenty-three lines to the page, but are frequently found with running titles and marginalia.

I also find that the lower-case fount in all these books is smaller than that used in printing the *Exhortation* of Erasmus which I referred to just now ; indeed, the number of lines to the page prove this, but whether it was the same type cut down or recast, I have not sufficient knowledge of type-founding to be able to say.

There are, of course, one or two books that will not fit in with this arrangement, as for instance, the *Ordinal or Statute*, printed for Richard Banckes, which has only twenty-two lines to the octavo page. It is just as well that it is so, because other books may come to light that tally with these exceptions, and so we shall be able in time to contract these two periods into smaller ones. I have put the year 1542 as the earliest year in the first period, because I find the *Questionary of Cyrurgeons* printed in Black Letter. But that work was a quarto, and there is no octavo that can be assigned to that year. It is quite possible, and even probable, that the octavo books were printed with 22 lines to the page, up to and including the year of the production of the *Ordinal*, that is about 1543 or 1544, but it hardly seems right to state so as a fact until other books turn up that are printed in the same way.

Another exception, which in no way affects the above classification was a book called *The 24 Stones* which was printed in a Black Letter unlike any other fount in the possession of this printer (type No. 7). It was a smaller and finer letter, making 27 lines to the octavo page, and was no doubt borrowed from some other printer for the occasion. This practice was very common among the early printers, and another of Wyer's books is a remarkable instance of it. His nearest neighbour was Richard Fawkes, who lived in Durham Rents, close to Durham House, and amongst the books printed by that printer was one entitled *De Cursione Lune.* It has Fawkes' colophon and device, but beneath them the words, "And be for to sell at the sign of St. John the Evangelist beside Charing Cross," which would of themselves be proof that it was printed for Robert Wyer. Not only is this put beyond doubt, but the fact is established that Wyer lent Fawkes the fount and the blocks to print it with, for when Wyer reprinted the book, with the "Suffolk" colophon, under the title of *The Nature of the Seven Days of the Week*, the type and blocks are identical with those used by Fawkes.

It does not seem, on the other hand, that Wyer ever printed anything for Fawkes. But he printed several books for Richard Banckes, at least one notable work for Richard Kele, who succeeded Bankes at the Long Shop in the Poultry, and one also for John Gough, who lived at the Mermaid, in Lombard Street.

Robert Wyer appears to have had a good stock of founts. In "Secretary" he had two at least, and they are generally found in combination. This type very closely resembles Caxton's type No. 4.

Of Black Letter types he had five or six founts, if not more, ranging from the Great Primer, a very beautiful letter seen at its best in Marshall's *Defence of Peace*, down to a very small lower-case letter, used for marginalia. He also had a fount of Roman capitals, a very poor one, chiefly used for initials. He was in the habit, especially in his later works, of using these types generously, and in the same title-page there will sometimes be found no less than five founts, four of them being Black Letter and one Secretary.

In the matter of initial letters also Wyer was especially rich, for he had a large and striking assortment. The most noticeable was a set of woodcut letters, adorned with grotesque faces. These so closely resemble some used by Wynkyn de Worde, that they may have belonged to the same set. Wyer does not appear to have had a complete alphabet of them, as he never used more than one or two in a single book. Another very fine set of capitals was an eight-line Roman, measuring 1¼ inches square, adorned with figures, animals and flowers. One of these, the letter " L," with the figure of a man dancing, is especially good; the pose of the figure is free and most artistic, and every detail of his dress is well shewn. This alphabet was also used by Wynkyn de Worde.

A third set of initial letters used by Robert Wyer was a text-hand, letter of German character. It occurs in Salisbury's *Description of the Worlde* (1550), and also in the *Dietary of Helthe.*

The most profusely illustrated of any of Robert Wyer's books was the *C. Hystoryes of Troy*, a translation made no doubt by Wyer himself, from Christine de Pisan's book with the same title, printed in Paris in 1490, by Philippe Pigouchet. In Wyer's book the woodcuts are copies from the pictures in the French edition. The first half-dozen or so are reversed, that is, the figures on the left of the original illustration, appear on the right in Wyer's reproduction, which would not have happened had the blocks been cut from the originals. As the French work is full of illustrations, many of them repeated, Wyer, in order to save the time and trouble of cutting duplicate blocks, used up any blocks he had by him, and I recognize several used in his other books, while some I have no doubt belong to books of which no copy is now to be found. For example, one of them represents the half-length of a woman in a pointed headgear and surrounded with stars, holding in her left hand a box or cradle, while on the left hand side of the block are the words "Lady Fortune." This was used in *The boke of the Fayre Gentylwoman, Lady Fortune,* of which the only copy known is in the Lambeth Palace Library. It figures again, with the title of "Lady Prudence, in *The Dispute between the Heralds of England and France,*" a book with Richard Wyer's colophon, though printed throughout with Robert's types and blocks.

The best example of engraving to be met with in Wyer's books is the printer's large device or book-plate. It represents the Evangelist seated on the ground writing, and on his right hand an eagle holding in his beak an ink-well. In the background is the view of a city. Beneath this was frequently put another block having the printer's name and mark. In addition to this, Wyer used a smaller block of the Evangelist, sometimes with the top portion cut away, sometimes with a border piece added to it; and almost invariably without the eagle. This was generally placed on the title-page or somewhere near it, while the large device is generally on the last page or below the colophon.

I mentioned just now "Richard" Wyer. There were three other printers or booksellers in London of the name of Wyer in the sixteenth century. Richard had a shop in St. Paul's Churchyard; John Wyer held what I believe to have been Butler's old shop in Fleet Street; and the third, Nicholas, is found at Charing Cross, at the same time as Thomas Colwell, that is, between 1562–1566. There is at present no evidence as to what relation these men bore to Robert Wyer. I am inclined to think that the two first were mere booksellers, because the few books which are found with their names prove to have been printed with Robert Wyer's types and blocks.

The third member of the group, Nicholas, stands on a different footing, and I hope we may be able to find out something more about him. It is evident that he was living at Charing Cross in 1556, and we must not be astonished at not finding any books printed by him before 1560. Queen Mary was then on the throne, and her reign, as we know, was disastrous to the printing trade, except to the firms which printed Roman Catholic books. Several of the printers, notably Richard Grafton, ceased to print and went abroad during her reign, and it may have been the same with Nicholas Wyer. It certainly looks as though he succeeded to the Charing Cross business, and afterwards took into partnership William Powell's apprentice, Thomas Colwell.

It now only remains for me to notice the character of the books that issued from the press of Robert Wyer.

The bulk of them were small octavos dealing with subjects of a popular nature, and therefore readily saleable. These remind us very forcibly that the people for whom they were intended, were grossly superstitious. Nearly every one of these little tracts deals with the influence of the weather, of the moon, of the planets, of precious stones, and of herbs, upon the health and destinies of mankind. No old wife's tale was too simple to be believed, and the wildest fables were repeated with all sincerity.

Religious feeling coloured the literature of the time very deeply, and we see the traces of it in the mass-books, diurnals, exhortations, and so forth, that form so large a part of Wyer's productions.

Medicine, again, was always in request ; hence the popularity of such works as the *Antidotarius*, and the translations from Arnaldus de Nova Villa and Ioannes de Vigo. In an age when physicians were few and costly, and the plague a frequent and dreaded visitor to all our great cities, books treating of the simplest and readiest cures were certain of a large sale.

Another popular book was *The Assize of Bread*, or "The Law of the Loaf," as it might be termed. Human nature was much the same then as it is now. Our County Council enforces the law that the poor shall not be cheated of their weight in coal, and four hundred years ago the State found it necessary to protect the poor against rascally bakers.

We are reminded again of this in the *Ordinal or Statutes* which regulated the employment of men and the wages they were to receive, and learn that such things as "sweating" and "strikes," long hours and short wages, were grievances then as now.

But all Wyer's publications were not for the cheap book stall. I have already referred to the *C. Hystoryes of Troy*. That book must have involved a considerable outlay and must have taken some considerable time to print, and it could only have been undertaken in the belief that the work when finished would attract the notice of wealthy buyers.

The *Defence of Peace* we now know cost £34 to print. William Marshall, the translator of it, wrote several books of a religious character. This one, however, was not a success. Though produced in the best possible way, it did not sell, and probably the printer as well as the author lost money over it.

Another book of importance was the *Questionary of Cyrurgeons*, printed at the costs of Robert Copland and Henry Dabb. This was a book not likely to have been sold for a few pence.

It is a noticeable thing that Wyer reprinted several parts of books that had previously issued from the press of Wynkyn de Worde. *The Medled Lyfe* was a series of extracts from *The Floure of the Commandements*. *The Properties of a Good Horse*, which he printed with the dialogue between Boccus and Sydrac, had previously appeared in the *Book of Hunting and Hawking*. I do not wish to attach undue importance to this. By itself it proves nothing, but it is worth bearing in mind, in connection with other things, as pointing to a possible business relationship between the two men.

I have now told you what I know about Robert Wyer and I believe you will agree with me that he was a printer of no mean order. It is evident that his brother craftsmen were of this opinion from the amount of work they gave him.

If he had done no more than print the *Defence of Peace* and the *Hystoryes of Troy*, he would well deserve a place amongst the first printers of his day. But much of his other work will bear comparison with what was done by others, while the number of books already traced to his press proves him to have been one of the busiest men in the trade.

ROBERT WYER'S TYPES.

No. 1.—*Secretary*, with lower-case letters *w*, *d* and *v* with a loop from left to right, making twenty-seven and twenty-eight lines to octavo page. Examples: *The Golden Pystle; Dyurnal of Devoute Soules; Interpretation of the Mass.*

   In one instance, *i.e., The Compost of Ptholomeus*, with the "Norwich" colophon, a larger *w*, having a double loop, is used with this type.

No. 2.—*Secretary*. Very much the same in character as above, but the lower-case letters *w*, *v* and *d* are not looped. Example : *The Defence of Peace* (1535).

   This type, I believe, continued to be used by Wyer during the whole of the time he printed, and the books found printed in "Secretary," with the "Suffolk" colophon, are in this type.

No. 3.—*Black Letter* (great primer). A fine and well-cut letter, used only for titles, colophons, and headings to subjects, etc. Seen at its best in *The Defence of Peace* (1535).

No. 4.—*Black Letter*. A large lower-case, four and a-half lines to inch, nineteen lines to page.

   The only two books I have seen, printed entirely in this type, are *The iiii Tokens*, by Jan van Doesborg, and *The Treatyse answerynge the Boke of Berdes*. It was generally used in combination with No. 5.

No. 5.—*Black Letter*. A smaller lower-case letter than the preceding, but well cut and regular.

First used in printing Erasmus's *Exhortation to the Study of the Scriptures* found with the "Norwich" colophon. It there makes twenty-one lines to octavo page. This type was afterwards very much cut down.

No. 6.—A very small *Black Letter*, used only for marginalia and supplementary matter.

No. 7.—*Black Letter.* A small, well-cut, and finer letter than either Nos. 4 or 5, making twenty-seven lines to octavo page.

I have found it in the *Boke of the XXIIII Stones*, and imagine it was borrowed by Wyer for that purpose, perhaps of Berthelet.

No. 8.—*Roman.* Capitals only.

INITIAL LETTERS.

1.—A set of woodcut initials, $\frac{13}{16}$ of an inch to an inch square, showing grotesque faces, sometimes used with a double rule and sometimes without. This may have been the same alphabet as that used by Wynkyn de Worde; but Wyer does not seem to have had a complete alphabet.

2.—A smaller set letters of the same character.

3.—A decorated roman, white on a black ground, ornamented with flowers, birds, animals and human beings. Size 1¼ inch square. Letters found in this—*F, I, L, O, S.* A letter *L* of this alphabet is to be found in the *New Herbal* of Macer, and is a very good example of this fine initial.

4.—A roman, 1$\frac{1}{16}$ inch square, with animals and human beings. Part of an alphabet only. Initial letters of this character were used by several other printers of that time, and came, it is believed, from Germany.

5.—A roman, white on a black ground, with floriated decoration.

6.—A roman, 1 inch square, ornamented, white on a stencilled background, sometimes showing flowers. Letters usually found—*R, T, W.*

7.—A roman, ¾ inch square, white on a black ground, with interlaced pattern.

8.—A roman, white on a black ground. Example: Letter *G* with a squirrel sitting upright.

9.—A text-hand initial, ⅝ of an inch square, found in books of a late date only, such as the *Description of the Sphere and Frame of the Worlde* (1550). Part of an alphabet only—*G, I, O, T, W.*

10.—A three-line Black Letter (great primer capital), ₇⁄₁₀ of an inch square.

11.—A set of roman capitals, very badly cut. Used sometimes for first line of title-page, as in Macer's *Herbal.*

These are some of the principal initials and capitals used by Wyer, but it is possible there are some others I have not seen.

DEVICES.

Robert Wyer's device consisted of a representation of St. John the Evangelist, bare-headed, and dressed in a long robe, seated under a tree, presumably in the Island of Patmos, writing on a scroll spread out on his knee. On the right hand side of him an eagle, with outstretched wings, holds in its beak an ink-well. Water appears to surround the spot on which the Evangelist is seated, and in the background is a view of a city with many towers and spires. Beneath this block is generally a smaller one, wedge-shaped, and having the printer's name and merchant's mark upon it. There were three forms of this device. 1. In the *Compost of Ptholomeus*, printed with the "Norwich" colophon, it appears on the verso of the last leaf in a much more crude state than in any other book. The name of the printer is cut on the same block as the device, and is spelt "Wyre," and the letters are straight, whereas in every other instance the name was cut in slanting letters. In the top left-hand corner of the block found in the *Compost*, the treatment of the upper part of the tree is altogether different from that found in any other example. It is also noticeable in this that the wavy lines representing water are not nearly so close in this as in the other form, and I believe it to be the earlier of the two. 2. The same device, but more clearly cut, and with the name-block separate. This is the one generally found in this printer's books, usually at the end.   Sometimes, but that rarely, the name-block only is inserted.   3. A smaller and mutilated form of No. 2, from which the eagle was omitted, and a geometrical side-piece introduced.   This is most usually found either on the title-page, or in the first part of a book.

WOODCUTS.

Next in importance to his devices are a set of small woodcuts, used singly, either on the title-page, or the verso of the title-page, and described by Herbert and others as "the figure with stars," "a three-quarter portrait," etc.   These are met with over and over again in Wyer's works. They were copied from a set of blocks used by Antoine Verard, the French printer, in his edition of the *Horae*, printed in 1490.

From whom Robert Wyer obtained them is, however, unknown, though several of his contemporaries had others of the same set.

As it may be interesting to some of my readers to identify these, I have made the following list:—

1.—Three-quarter figure with four stars. (*Horæ*, b⁵ verso)

2.—Three-quarter figure with hat and feather. (*Horæ*, b⁸ recto.)

3.—Lady with pointed head-gear. (*Horæ*, a *ij* recto.)

4.—Three-quarter figure of a man looking to the left, through a window. (*Horæ*, a *i* verso.)

5.—Lady with candle in right hand. (*Horæ*, a *j* verso second leaf.)

6.—Lady with rose. (*Horæ*, a *j* recto of second leaf.)

7.—Crucifixion. (*Horæ*, l *ij* recto.)

The next most important series of blocks were those which Wyer cut himself for his edition of the *C. Hystoryes of Troy*, probably printed about 1543 or 1545. Some of the blocks cut for this book he used in others; amongst them the *Castell of Love,* and the *Questions of King Boccus,* which are thereby proved to have been printed at a later date.

Another woodcut often met with in Wyer's books is that representing Ptolemy and female figures, the philosopher having a mathematical instrument in his left hand. This measures $2\frac{11}{16} \times 2\frac{12}{16}$ inch, and appears in most of the geographical and astronomical tracts.

The title-page of the *Assize of Bread* is adorned with four blocks illustrating the trade of a baker.

The *Perfyte Prognostication* has a series of woodcuts which might have been conceived and executed by a small boy with a blunt pen-knife.

LIST OF WYER'S BOOKS.

DIVISION I.

BOOKS WITH "NORWICH" COLOPHON, OR WITH DATES EARLIER THAN 1536.

1.—ST. BERNARD. *The Golden Pystle*, 1531. 8vo.

COLLATION: a–b, in fours; 8 ff.; 28 ll. Types 1, 3 and 5.

DESCRIPTION: [*Title*] Here begynneth ‖ a goodly treatyfe/ and it is called ‖ a notable leffon,' otherwyfe it ‖ is called the golden pyflle ‖ Imprynted in the yere ‖ of oure lorde god M‖CCCCC.xxxi. ‖ [*Device No. 3.*]

    Colophon : ℂ Imprynted by me Robert Wyre, dwellynge at the sygne of seynt Iohan euangelyft in seynt Martyns paryffhe in the felde befyde Charynge croffe in the byffhop of Norwytche rentys. [*Device No. 2.*]

COPY: British Museum (C. 40, a. 25).

2.—GARARDE. *Interpretacyon of the Maffe*, 1532. 8vo.

COLLATION: ✠ 4 leaves; a–z, in fours; & 4 leaves; A–E, in fours; 120 ff., 28 ll. Types 1, 3 and 5.

DESCRIPTION: [*Title*] The interpreta‖cyon/ and syg-‖nyfycacyon of ‖ the Maffe, ‖ ℂ Here begynneth a good deuoute ‖ Boke to the honoure of god/ of our lady ‖ his mother/ and of all fayntes, and ryght ‖ profytable to all good Catholyke per-‖fones,' to knowe howe they fhall de-‖uoutly here Maffe . And how falu‖taryly they fhal confeffe them . ‖ And how reuerently and honourably they ‖ fhall go to the holy facrament or table ‖ of our fauyour Ihefu chryfte/ With dy-‖uerfe other profytable documents and ‖ orayfons or prayers here conteyned/ ‖ Compofed and ordeyned by frere ‖ Gararde/ frere mynoure/ of the ‖ ordre of the Obfervauntes . ‖

   Colophon: ☞ Imprynted by me Robert Wyer/ dwel-‖lynge at the fygne of faynt Iohn̄ Euā-‖gelyfte/ in faynt Martyns paryffhe ‖ in the felde/ in the Byffhop of ‖ Norwytche rentes befy‖de Charynge croffe . ‖ ☞ In the yere of our Lorde God a M . ‖ CCCCC . xxxii . The viii daye ‖ of the moneth of Octobre ‖ ☞ Cum Priuilegio Regali : pro fpatio feptem annorum . [*Device No. 2.*]

COPY: British Museum (C. 25, c. 21).

2A.—HAEMMERLEIN, THOMAS À KEMPIS. *Folowyng of Chryfte.* *n.d.* 8vo.

COLLATION : a–h, in fours.

DESCRIPTION : [*Title*] Here after foloweth the fourth boke, of the folowyng of Chryfte, which treateth moste specyally of the Sacrament of the aulter.

   Colophon : Imprynted by me Robert wyer dwellynge at the sygne of saynte Iohan Euangelyste, in saynt Martyns parysshe, in the bysshop of Norwytche rentes besyde Charynge crosse . [1535 ?] 8vo.

COPY: Private Library.

3.—LARKE, IOHN. *Boke of wysdome,* 1532. 12mo.

COLLATION : 68 ff. Type 1 or 3.

DESCRIPTION : [*Title*] ☞ The boke of wysdome, folowynge the auctoryties of auncyent Phylosophers Dyuydynge/ and spekyng of vyces and vertues/ wherby a man may be praysed, or dysprayfed with the maner to speke alwayes well and wysely to all folkes . / of what eftate so euer they be. [*Cut.*]

   Colophon : Here endith the boke of wysdom after the sayenges of auncyent Phylosophers and other noble wyse men/ lately translated out of French into Englyffhe . ☞ Imprynted by ——— in Saynt Martyns paryffhe befyde Charynge Croffe . The yere of our Lorde god . M . CCCCC and XXXII . the XX day of Ianuarie ☞ Cum priuilegio Regali pro fpatio septem annorum.

NOTES: The above description is taken from Herbert's edition of *Ames' Typographical Antiquities*, Vol. 1, p. 369. The work was a translation from the French of an Italian book, called the *Fior di Virtù*, first printed about 1470.

C 2

4.—Marshall, W.   *The Defence of Peace,* 1535.   Folio.

Collation: a–c, in sixes; d 5 leaves; e–z, in sixes; & 4 leaves; 141 ff.,
    50 ll.   Types 2, 3 and 5.

Description: [*Title*] The Defence of Peace: late-||ly tranſlated out of la-||ten
    in to englyſſhe . || [*Coat of Arms.*] ☾ with the kynges moſte || gracyous
    priuilege.

> *Colophon:* Prynted by me Robert wyer/ || for wyllyam marſhall/
> and || fynyſſhed in the moneth of || Iuly in the yere of our Lorde god a
> M . || CCCCC . || xxxv . || And in the xxvii . yere of the Reygne of our
> moſte || gracyous foucraygne lorde Henry the eyght, || by the grace of
> god, of Englande, and of || Fraunce, kynge, defender of the || fayth, and
> lorde of Irelande/ || and fupreme hed vnder || god of the churche || of
> Englande . || With the priuilege of our || moſte gracious foue-||raygne
> Lorde/ || for ſixe yeres. [*Device No. 2.*], Fo. 141ᵃ, Fo. 141ᵇ [*Coat of
> Arms.*]

Copies: British Museum (475, c. 2); Lambeth Library.

Remarks: Robert Wyer's Great Primer type is seen at its best in this book.   Altogether, it
    may be classed as the best specimen of his work.

5.—Bustarde, A.   *Cessyons of Parlyment.   n.d.*   4to.

Collation: a–g, in fours; 28 ff.

Description : [*Title*] The Cessyōs or Parlyamēt of the imperyall Realme of
    Englande . And the assemblaunce of the same.   [Verso, *Device No. 3.*]

> *Colophon:* Tranſlated out of latyn in to Englyſſhe by one Antony
> Bustarde, felowe of Lyons Inne . Imprynted by me Robert Wyer,
> dwellynge in saynte Martyns parysshe, in the bysshope of Norwythche
> rentes . Cum priu., etc.   [*Device No. 2.*]

Reference: Dibdin, Vol. 3, p. 212.

6.—*Complaint of a dolorous lover.   n.d.* [c. 1536].   4to.

Collation : A, four leaves.   Type 5.

Description : [*Title*] ☾ Here begynneth a complaynt of a dolorous Lover,
    upon sugred wordes || and fayned coūntenaūnce . || ☾ I say in ryght is

reason ‖ in trust is treason . The love of a woman ‖ doth laste but a season . ‖ Robert ‖ Wyer the ‖ Prynter.   [The last four words surrounded by four border pieces.]

   Colophon : Imprynted by me Robert Wyer dwellynge at the sygne of saynt Iohn̄ Evangelyſt ‖ in saynt Martyns paryſſhe, beſyde charyng croſſe, in norwytch rents . ‖ ℂ Cum priuilegio regali.   [*Device No. 2.*]

COPY : Huth Library.

7.—*Compost of Ptholomeus.   n.d.* [c. 1532].   8vo.

COLLATION : a–r, in fours ; 68 ff. ; 28 ll.   Types 1, 3 and 5.

DESCRIPTION : [*Title*] Here begynneth ‖ The Compoſt of Ptholomeus/ ‖ Prynce of Aſtronomye : Tran‖ſlated oute of Frenche in to ‖ Englyſſhe/ for them that ‖ wolde haue knowlege ‖ of the Compoſt. [*Woodcut.*]   Fo. 1ᵇ [*Coat of Arms* as in the *First Dyaloge.*]

   Colophon : ℂ Imprynted by me Robert Wyer/ Dwel-,lynge at the fygne of feynt Iohn̄ Euan-‖gelyſte/ in feynt Martyns Paryſſhe in ‖ the felde/ in the byſſhop of Norwyt‖che rentes/ besyde Charyng croſſe. [*Device No. 1.*]

COPY : British Museum (717, a. 5).

8.—*Diurnal.   n.d.* [c. 1532].   8vo.

COLLATION : a–b, in fours ; c two leaves ; 10 ff. ; 27 ll.   Types 1, 3 and 5.

DESCRIPTION : [*Title*] ℂ A dyurnall : ‖ for deuoute foulles : to ordre ‖ them felfe ‖ therafter. [*Device No. 3.*]

   Colophon : Imprynted by me Robert wyer/ dwel-‖lynge at the Sygne of faynt Iohan ‖ Euangelyſt/ in faynt Martyns ‖ paryſſhe in the byſſhop of ‖ Norwytche rentes ‖ befyde charyn-‖ge Croſſe. [Verso of C. 2. Cum priuilegio Regali : pro ‖ ſpatio feptem annorum . ‖ . ˙ . ‖ ℂ And be for to fell at the fygne ‖ of faynt Iohn̄ Euangelyſte. *Device No. 2.*]

COPY : British Museum (C. 25, d. 9).

9.—Erasmus. *Exhortation. n.d.* 8vo.

Collation : a–i, in eights ; 72 ff. ; 21 ll.   Types 1, 3 and 5.

Description : [*Title*] An exhorta-‖cyon to the dy‖lygent study ‖ of scripture : ‖ made by Erafmus of Roterodamus, ‖ And lately tranflated into ‖ Englyffhe . [Verso of d ij, *Device 3.*] d iij recto, ℭ An exhorta-‖cyon to the ‖ study of ‖ the ‖ Gofpell/ ‖ Made by Erafmus of ‖ Roterodame, & lately ‖ tranflated in to ‖ Englyffhe.

> *Colophon :* Imprynted ‖ by me Robert wyer, dwel-‖lyng in Saynt Martyns ‖ paryffhe, in the byf-‖fhoppe of Nor-‖wytche ren-‖tes.   Recto of j viii . [*Coat of Arms*] similar to those in the *Fyrft Dyaloge* and the *Compost of Ptholomeus.* [*Device No. 2.*]

Copy : British Museum (C. 27, a. 31, 1).

Remarks : This is the best specimen of Wyer's Black Letter.

10.—*Jordans medytacyons. n.d.* 8vo.

Collation : a–g, in fours.

Description : [*Title*] Jordans medytacyons, with other dyuers matters in Englyffhe : as apyeryth by a short Table in the ende/ after the ordre of the Λ . B . C.   [*Cut.*]

> *Colophon :* Imprynted by me ——— in the byffhop of Norwytches rentes . — Cum priuilegio Regali pro fpatio feptem annorum.

Reference : Herbert, Vol. 1, p. 383.

Note : This was a translation of *Jordanus de Quedlinburg.*

11.—*Notable Chapters. n.d.* 8vo.

Collation : a–c, in eights.

Description : [*Title*] ℭ Here ben cõteyned fiue notable Chapytres : moche profytable for euery man, dylygently to recorde . And after do folowe thyrtene degrees of Morty fycacyon.   [*Cut.*]

> *Colophon :* Imprynted by me ——— in the byffhop of Norwytches rentes. [*Device No. 2.*]

Reference : Herbert, Vol. 1, p. 382.

12.—*Ordinances of Charles V.* n.d. [c. 1532]. 8vo.

COLLATION : Λ–C, in fours ; D, eight leaves with double signatures ; E–L, in fours ; 48 ff ; 25 ll.   Types 1, 3 and 5.

DESCRIPTION : [*Title*] Thefe ben ‖ the ordynañces that ‖ the Emperour hath caufed ‖ to be red and declared in his prefence,' to ‖ theftates of his countrees of thofe par-‖tyes at theyr affemblynge to his ma-‖geftye the vii day of Octobre,' the ‖ yere of our Lorde . M V . C . xxxi . ‖ The whiche haue be publyf-‖fhed through all the fayd ‖ countrees the xv day ‖ of Novembre folowynge,' as well to the ‖ auoydynge of the Lutheran fecte' ‖ and other reproued fectes, as for ‖ pourucyaûnce of the dyfor-‖dre of his Coyne' & ordres ‖ to be fette in the fayde ‖ Countrees . ‖ ℭ Cum priuilegio Regali.

    Colophon : ℭ Imprynted by me Robert ‖ wyer, dwellynge at the fy-‖gne of faynt Iohñ Evā-‖ngelyft' i faynt Mar-‖tyns paryffhe in ‖ the byffhop of Norwytche ‖ rentes befyde Cha-‖rynge Croffe. [Verso of last leaf, *Device No. 2.*]

COPY : Bodleian Library.

13.—ST. GERMAIN. *Fyrfte dyaloge in Englyffhe.* n.d. [c. 1531]. 8vo.

COLLATION : a–u, in fours ; 80 ff. ; 27 ll.   Types 1, 3 and 5.

DESCRIPTION : [*Title*] The fyrfte dya-‖loge in Englyf-‖fhe,' with newe addycyons. [*Coat of Arms* as in No. 10.]

    Colophon : Imprynted by me Robert wyer ‖ dwellynge at the fygne of faynt ‖ Iohñ Euangelyfte, in faynt ‖ Martyns paryffhe' befyde ‖ Charyngcroffe' in the Byf‖fhop of norwych rentes. [*Device No. 2.*]

COPIES : British Museum (506, a. 2) ; U. L. C.

14.—SYLVESTER, BERNARD. *Cure and Gouernance of a Houfehold.* n.d. 8vo.

COLLATION : Λ–B, in fours ; 8 ff.

DESCRIPTION : [*Title*] Here begynneth a fhort monycyon, or counfayle of the cure and gouernaunce of a houfholde,' accordynge vnto policy : taken out of a pyftle of a great learned man/ called Bernarde sylveftre. [*Device No. 3.*]

    Colophon : Here endeth the boke Intituled the gouernaunce of a houfholde . Imprynted by me Robert Wyer in the byfhop of Norwytche rentes befyde charynge Croffe. [*Device No. 2.*]

REFERENCE : Herbert's edition of *Ames*, Vol. 1, p. 384.

DIVISION II.

BOOKS WITH "SUFFOLK" COLOPHON.

15.—ARISTOTLE. *Nature of the Days of the Week. n.d.* 8vo.

COLLATION: A–B, in eights; 16 ff.; 27 ll. Types 2 and 3

DESCRIPTION: [*Title*] Here begyn-||neth the Nature, and Dyſpoſy-||cyen of the dayes of the weke, and || ſheweth what the Thondre in || euery Moneth in the yere, || chaunſynge, doth pro-||tende and fygnyfye/ || with the courſe and dyſpoſycyon, || of the dayes of the Moone : whi-||che be good, and whiche be || badde : after the influ-||entes of the Moone/ || drawen out of a || laten Boke of || Ariſtotiles de || Aſtronomis. [*Cut.*]

    Colophon: ℂ Imprinted by me Robert wyer/ dwel:||lynge at the ſygne of ſaynt Iohn̄ euā||gelyſt, in ſaynt Martyns paryſſhe || in the Duke of Suffolkes ren-||tes.' beſyde charynge || Croſſe. [*Name block only.*]

COPY: British Museum (C. 20, a. 34).

REMARKS: This was a reprint of the book entitled *De Curſione Lune*, printed by R. Fawkes for Robert Wyer.

16.—[Another edition.]

COLLATION: A–B, in eights.

DESCRIPTION: Here Begynneth the Nature and Dyspoſycion of the vij dayes in the Weke, and sheweth what the Thondre in euery Month in the yere, chaunsynge, doth protende and Sygnyfye . With the course and Dyspoſycion of the dayes of the Moone, whiche ben good, and which ben bad after the Influentes of the Moone . Drawen oute of a laten Booke of Aristotiles de Astronimis.

    Colophon: Imprinted by me Robert Wyer . Dwellynge at the sygne of S. Iohn̄ Euangelyſt in S. Martyns Parysshe, in the Duke of Suffolkes rentes besyde Charynge Crosse.

COPY: Private Library.

17.—*Assize of Bread.* *n.d.* [c. 1545]. 4to.

COLLATION : A–D, in fours ; 16 ff. ; 32 and 33 ll. Types 3, 4 and 5.

DESCRIPTION : [*Title*] ❡ Here begynneth the Boke ‖ named the Aſſyſe of Breade: what it ought to weye ‖ after the Pryce of a quarter of Wheete . And al-‖ſo the Aſſyſe of Ale, with all maner of woode ‖ & Cole; Lath; Bowrde/ and tymbre, and ‖ and the weyght of Buttre/ and Cheſe . ‖ Imprinted by me Robert Wyer. [*Cut.*]

Colophon : Imprynted by me Robert wyer : dwellynge ‖ in ſaynet martyns paryſhe, beſyde Cha-‖rynge Croſſe, at the ſygne of sanycte ‖ Iohñ Euangelyſt beſyde the ‖ Duke of Suffolkes ‖ place. [*Name block only.*]

COPY : British Museum (C. 38, d. 2).

REMARKS : Reference is made in this to a statute that was to take effect from 1543.

18.—*Boke of Demaundes.* *n.d.* 8vo.

COLLATION : A–D, in fours ; 16 ff.

DESCRIPTION : [*Title*] The Boke of Demaundes, of the scyence of Phylosophye and Astronomye, Betwene kynge Boctus, and the Phylosopher Sydracke.

Colophon : Imprinted by me Robert Wyer, dwellynge in the Duke of Suffolkes Rentes besyde charynge Crosse.

COPY : Private Library.

REMARKS : The title and colophon as given by Dibdin do not agree with this and may refer to another edition.

19.—*Boke of the fayre Gentylwoman.* *n.d.* 8vo.

COLLATION : A–B, in fours ; 8 ff. Types 2, 3 and 4.

DESCRIPTION : [*Title*] ❡ The Boke of the fayre Gentyl‖woman, that no man ſhulde ‖ put his truste, or confy‖dence in : that is to ſay, ‖ Lady Fortune ; ‖ flaterynge euery man ‖ that coueyteth to ‖ haue all, and specyally ‖ them that truste in ‖ her, she deccy‖ueth them ‖ at laste. [*Cut.*]

Colophon : Imprynted by me Robert wyer dwellinge in Saynt Martyns paryſſe, (*sic.*) in the Duke of Suffolkes rentes, besyde Charynge Croſſe . Ad imprimendum solum.

COPY: Lambeth Library, Maitland's Early Printed Books in the Lambeth Library, p. 439, *et seq.*

20.—*Boke of Knowledge.* *n.d.* 8vo.

COLLATION : A, in fours ; B, two ; 6 ff. ; 27 ll. Types 2, 3 and 4.

DESCRIPTION : [*Title*] ❡ The Boke of ‖ Knowledge ‖ whether a ſycke perſon ‖ beynge in perylle ‖ ſhall lyue, or ‖ dye . etc . ‖ ✠ [*Cut.*]

 Colophon : Imprynted by ‖ me Robert wyer : dwellyn-ge at the ſygne of ſaynte ‖ Iohñ Euangelyſte in ‖ ſaynt Martyns Pa-‖ryſſhe,/ in the Duke ‖ of Suffolkes ren-‖tes befyde ‖ Charynge Crosse . ‖ ✠ [*Device No. 2.*]

COPY : British Museum (C. 40, a. 29).

21.—BORDE, ANDREW. *Boke for to lerne a man to be wyſe.* *n.d.* 8vo.

COLLATION : A-D, in fours ; 16 ff. ; 25 ll. Types 2, 3, 4 and 6.

DESCRIPTION : [*Title*] The boke for to ‖ Lerne a man to be wyfe in ‖ buyldyng of his howſe for ‖ the helth of body & to hol-de quyetnes for the helth ‖ of his foule, and body . ‖ ❡ The boke for a good ‖ huſbande to learne. [*Cut*, round which is the following]: "we Mayſters of Aſtronomye, And doctoures in Phefycke, cõfyrmeth this fayenge to be good & trewe both for the body, and alfo for the foule."

 Colophon : Imprynted by me Robert ‖ wyer, dwellynge at the ſygne of S . ‖ Iohñ Euangelyſt, in s . Martyns ‖ paryſſhe in the felde befyde the ‖ Duke of Suffolkes pla-ce at Charynge ‖ Croſſe . ‖ Cum priuilegio, Ad ‖ imprimendum ‖ solum.

COPY : British Museum (C. 40, a. 24).

22.—BENESE, RICHARD. *Measuring of Land.* *n.d.* 8vo.

COLLATION : A-G, in eights ; 56 ff. ; 23 and 25 ll. Types 2, 3, 4 and 5.

DESCRIPTION : [*Title*] This Boke ‖ Newely Imprynted, ‖ sheweth the maner of ‖ meafuryng of all maner of ‖ Lande, as well of woodlande, ‖ as of Plowelande, and Paf-‖tour in the Felde, & comp-‖tynge the true nombre ‖ of Acres of the ‖ fame . ‖ ℂ Newely inuented and ‖ compyled by Syr Richar-‖de Benefe . Chanon of ‖ Marton Abbay be‖fyde London.

> *Colophon :* Imprynted by me Robert ‖ Wyer dwellynge in the Duke of ‖ Suffolkes rentes, befyde ‖ Charynge Croffe.

COPY : British Museum (530, a. 14).

NOTE : This was merely an abridgement of the *Measuring of Land*, which was first printed by Nicholson in Southwark, without date, but about 1537.

23.—*Mappa Mundi.   n.d.*   8vo.

COLLATION : A–C, in fours ; 12 ff. ; 23 ll.   Types 3, 4 and 5.

DESCRIPTION : [*Title*] Mappa Mundi, ‖ Otherwyfe called the Com-‖paffe, and Cyrcuet of the ‖ worlde, and alfo the Com-‖paffe of euery Ilande, ‖ comprehendyd in ‖ the same.   [*Cut.*]

> *Colophon :* ℂ Imprinted by me ⅅ ‖ Robert wyer, dwellynge in s. Mar-‖tyns paryffhe, at the fygne of ‖ S . Iohñ Euangelyft, befyde ‖ the Duke of Suffolkes ‖ places, at charynge ‖ Croffe . ‖ Cum priuilegio, ad impri‖mendum folum.   [Verso of C, 4, *Device No. 2.*]

COPY : British Museum (717, a. 49.)

24.—PISAN (CHRISTINE DE).   *One Hundred Histories of Troye.   n.d.*   8vo.

COLLATION : A–U, in eights ; 20 and 24 ll. to pages.   Types : Title—Nos. 3 and 2 ; Text—Nos. 2, 4, 5 and 6.

DESCRIPTION : [*Title*] ℂ Here foloweth ‖ the C . Hyftoryes ‖ of Troye . ‖ [*Cut*] Lepiftre de Othea deeffe de Prudence/ ‖ enuoyee a lefperit cheualereux Hector ‖ de Troye, auec cent Hiftoires . ‖ Nouuellement imprimeé.

> *Colophon :* Imprynted by me Robert ‖ wyer, dwelling in S . Mar‖tyns paryffhe, at charynge Croffe . ‖ at the fygne of s . Iohñ Euan-‖gelift befyde the Duke of ‖ Suffolkes place.   [*Name block only.*]

COPY : British Museum (C. 31, a. 24).

REMARKS : The most copiously illustrated of all Wyer's books.   Most of the blocks were copies from the illustrations in the French edition.

25.—*Prognostication of Erra Pater.* *n.d.* 8vo.

COLLATION: A–B, in eights; 16 ff.; 24 ll.   Types 2, 3, 4, 5 and 6.

DESCRIPTION: [*Title*] The ‖ Pronoſtycacion ‖ For euer of Erra Pater : ‖ A
    Iewe borne in Iewery, a ‖ Doctour in Aſtronomye, ‖ and Phyſycke .
    Profyta‖ble to kepe the bodye ‖ in helth . And alſo ‖ Ptholomeus ſayth ‖
    the ſame . ‖ Erra Pater . ‖ [*Cut*] This Pronoſtycacion ſer-‖ueth for all the
    world ouer.

> *Colophon :* Imprynted by me Robert ‖ Wyer, dwellynge at the ſygne
> of ‖ S . Iohn Euangelyſte, in S . Mar-‖tyns paryſſhe, in the Duke of
> Suf-‖folkes rentes, beſyde charynge ‖ Croſſe.   [*Name block only.*]

COPY: British Museum (C. 40, a. 32).

25A.—*Prognostycacion of two Shepherdes.* *n.d.* 8vo.

COLLATION: A–B, in fours; 8 ff.

DESCRIPTION: [*Title*] Prognostycacion & Almanacke of two Shepherdes
    necessarye for all Housholders .   [*Cut.*]

> *Colophon :* Imprynted by me Robert Wyer, dwellynge in Seynt
> Martyns paryſſhe in the Duke of Suffolkes rentes, beſyde Charynge
> Crosse.

REFERENCE: Dibdin, *Typ. Antiq.*, Vol. 3, p. 197.

REMARKS: On the last page is an Almanacke for Anno M . d . l vi.   I fancy this colophon
    must have been reprinted from an earlier edition as the house had long since passed out
    of the possession of the Dukes of Suffolk.

26.—PTOLEMY.   *Compost of Ptholomeus.* *n.d.* 8vo.

COLLATION: A–S, in fours; 72 ff.; 27 ll.   Types 2, 3, 4 and 5.

DESCRIPTION: [*Title*] The Compost of ‖ Ptholomeus/ Prince of ‖ Aſtronomye,
    Tranſlated out ‖ of Frenche in to Englyſſhe For ‖ euery Perſon/ that
    wolde ‖ haue knowledge of ‖ the Com-‖poſt.

Colophon : ⫷ Imprinted by me Robert ‖ Wyer Dwellynge at the fygne of ‖ feynt Iohñ Euangelyft, in feynt ‖ Martyns paryffhe, in the Duke ‖ of Suffolkes Rentes be-‖fyde Charynge ‖ Croffe . ‖ ⫷ Cum priuilegio, ad ‖ imprimendum folum.

COPY : British Museum (717, a. 44).

REMARKS : This was a reprint of the edition of 1531, with the addition of a " Rutter of the dyftaunces from one Porte or Coun-‖tree to another," which occupies from the Verso of S, ii to Verso of S, 4. There is no clue to the translator of this Compost.

27.—VIGO (I. DE). *Lytell Practyce. n.d,* 8vo.

COLLATION : A–B, in eights ; 16 ff. ; 24 ll. Types 3, 4 and 5.

DESCRIPTION : [*Title*] This lytell Prac-‖tyce of Iohãnes ‖ de Vigo in Medycyne/ is ‖ tranflated out of Laten ‖ in to Englyffhe/ for ‖ the health of the ‖ body of man. [*Device No. 3,* and round it] : "These Medycynes were ‖ proued by Thortone."

Colophon : Imprynted by me Robert ‖ wyer : dwellynge befyde ‖ Suffolkes place/ at ‖ charynge Croffe.

COPY : British Museum (C. 31, a. 35).

DIVISION III.

BOOKS UNCLASSIFIED.

28.—*Antidotharius.   n.d.   8vo.*

COLLATION : A–E, in fours ; 20 ff. ; 27 ll.   Types 2, 3, 4 and 5.

DESCRIPTION : [*Title*] The Antido-‖tharius, in the whiche thou mayst ler-‖ne howe thou ſhalt make many and dyvers ‖ noble playſters, ſalues, oyntementes pow-‖ders, bawmes, oyles, and wounde dryn-‖kes, the whiche be verye neccssarye ‖ and behouefull, utyle and prof-‖ytable for everye Sur-‖gyan therin to be ‖ excpert, and redy at all ‖ tymes of nede. [*Device No. 3.*   With a border piece.]

    Colophon : Imprymted (*sic*) by me Robert Wyer ‖ dwellyng at the sygne of saynt Iohn̄ ‖. Evangelyſt in saynt Martyns ‖ parysshe besyde Cha-‖rynge Crosse.   [Verso of E, 4, *Device No. 2.*]

COPY : British Museum (C. 31, a. 16).

29.—*Antidotharius.   n.d.   8vo.*

COLLATION : A–E, in fours ; 20 ff. ; 27 ll.   Types 2, 3, 4 and 5.

DESCRIPTION : [*Title*] The Antido-‖tharius, in the which thou mayſt ler-‖ne howe thou ſhalte make many, and dyuers ‖ noble playſters, ſalues, oyntementes, pow-‖ders, bawmes, oyles, and wounde dryn-‖kes, the whiche be verye neceſſarye, ‖ and behouefull, vtyle and pro-‖fytable for euerye Sur-‖gyan, therin to be ‖ experte, and redy all ‖ tymes of nede. [*Device No. 3.*   With a border piece.]

    Colophon : Imprynted by me Robert ‖ Wyer : Dwellynge at the ſygne of ‖ S. Iohn̄ Euangelyſt, in ſaynt ‖ Martyns paryſſhe : beſyde ‖ Charynge Croſſe.   [*Device No. 2.*]

COPY : British Museum (C. 31, a. 37).

30.—*Antidotharius. n.d.* 8vo.

COLLATION: a–e, in fours; 20 ff. ; 27 ll.   Types 2, 3, 4 and 5.

DESCRIPTION: [*Title*] The Antido-||tharius, in the whiche thou mayſt || lerne howe thou ſhalte make many, || and dyuers noble plaſters, ſalues, || oyntemět, powders, bawmes, || oyles . & wounde drynkſſ/ the || whiche be very neceſſary, || and behouefull || vtyle/ & profytable, || for euery Surgyan, therin || to be expert/ and redy at || all tymes of nede.   [*Device No. 3.*]

    Colophon: Imprynted by me Robert wyer/ dwel-||lynge at yᵉ ſygne of ſaynt Iohñ cuan||gelyſte/ in ſaynt Martyns paryſ-||ſhe/ beſyde Charynge croſſe.   [*Device No. 2.*]

COPY: British Museum (C. 31, a. 31).

31.—ARNALDUS DE VILLA NOVA. *Defence of Age. n.d.* 8vo.

COLLATION: A–B, in fours; 8 ff. ; 24 ll.   Type 2, 3, 4 and 5.

DESCRIPTION: [*Title*] ℂ Here is a newe || Boke, called the defence of age/ || and recoury of youth/ tranſla||ted out of the famous Clarke || and ryght experte medy-||cyne Arnold de Noua || Villa/ very profyta-||ble for all men || to knowe.   [*Device No. 3.*]   Verso of title page;   Dedication by Jonas Drumunde to "Lady Margaret Douglas," daughter of the Earl of Angus, niece of Henry 8th and sister to Iames "kynge of Scottes".

    Colophon: Imprynted by me Robert || wyer/ dwellynge in ſaynt || Martyns paryſſhe/ at || the ſygne of ſaynt || Iohñ Euangelyſt/ || beſyde Charyn-||ge Croſſe . || ⊬   [*Name block only.*]

COPY: British Museum (1165, b. 24).

REMARKS: K. James of Scotland died in 1542.

32.—ARNALDUS DE VILLA NOVA. *Defence of Age. n.d.* 8vo.

COLLATION: Two sheets.

DESCRIPTION: [*Title*] Here is a newe boke called the defence of age, and re-covery of youth translated by the famous clarke, and ryght expert doctor of medycyne Arnold de Noua Villa, very profytable for all men to know.

REFERENCE: Herbert, Vol. 1, p. 381.

REMARKS: This may be the same as the preceding.

33.—*Ars Moriendi.* *n.d.* 12mo.

DESCRIPTION : [*Title*] Ars Moriendi . Here begynneth a lytell treatyse
shortlye compyled and called Ars Moriendi, that is to saye the crafte to
dye, For the helth of mannes soule.

    Colophon : Imprinted by Robert Wyer. [*Woodcut.*]

COPY : Private Library.

34.—*Assize of Bread.* *n.d.* 4to.

COLLATION : A–D, in fours ; 16 ff. ; 33 ll.   Types 2, 3 and 5.

DESCRIPTION : [*Title*] ¶ Here begynneth the boke ‖ named the Affyfe of
Breade,' what it ought to ‖ weye,' after the Pryce of a quarter of wheete . ‖
And alfo the Affyfe of Ale, with all maner ‖ of woode and cole,' lath/
bowrde,' tymbre,' and the weyght of Butyre,' and Chefe . ‖ Imprynted by
me Robert wyer. [*Cut.*]

    Colophon : Imprynted by me Robert wyer, ‖ Dwellynge in feynt
Martyns ‖ paryffhe at Charynge croffe . ‖ at the Sygne of feynt ‖ Iohñ
Euangelyft. [*Device No. 2.*]

COPY : British Museum (C. 38, d. 3).

35.—*Beaulte of Women.* *n.d.* 8vo.

COLLATION : Six leaves only.

DESCRIPTION : [*Title*] This Boke is named the beaulte of women translated
out of frenche into Englyffhe. [*Cut.*]

    Colophon : Imprynted by me Robert Wyer, dwellynge in Saynt
Martyns paryffhe at the fygne of faynt Iohñ Euängelyft befýde Charynge
Croffe. [*Device No. 2.*]

REFERENCE : Dibdin, Vol. 3, pp. 210, 211.

36.—BACON, ROGER. *Boke of Waters.* *n.d.* 8vo.

COLLATION : A–B, in fours ; C, six leaves ; 14 ff. ; 24 ll.   Types 3, 4, 5 and 6.

DESCRIPTION : [*Title*] ⟨ This Boke doth ‖ treate all of the beste waters Artyfycialles/ ‖ and the ver‖tues and properties of the ‖ same moche profytable ‖ for the poor sycke, set ‖ forth by Sir Roger ‖ Becon Freere. [*Device No. 3.*]

Colophon : Imprynted by me Robert wyer.

COPY : British Museum (C. 31, a. 30).

37.—BECON, THOMAS. *Antithesis. n.d.* 8vo.

DESCRIPTION : [*Title*] Antithesis, wherein the word of God and mans inuentions are compared.

REFERENCE : Herbert, Vol. 1, p. 379.

38.—BECON, THOS. *Shield of Salvation. n.d.* 8vo.

COLLATION : A–H, in eights ; 64 ff.

DESCRIPTION : [*Title*] The Shelde of Saluacion . Newely fette forthe in Englyffhe, to the greate comfort of all faythfull penytent fynners . Psal 61 . God onely is my ftrength, my faluation and defence, fo that I fhall not fall . In God is my health, my glorye, my myghte, yea in God is all my trufte.

Colophon : Imprynted by me ———— dwellynge befyde Charynge Croffe . Ad imprimendum folum. [*Device No. 2.*]

REFERENCE : Herbert, Vol. 1, p. 378.

39.—*Boccus and Sydrac. n.d.* 8vo.

COLLATION : A–C, in fours ; 12 ff. ; 23 ll. Types 2, 3, 4, 5 and 6.

DESCRIPTION : [*Title*] ⟨ Here be Cer-‖tayne Queftyons of Kyn-‖ge Bocthus of the maners/ ‖ tokyns and condycions ‖ of man/ with the an-‖fweres made to ‖ the fame by ‖ the Phylo-‖fopher ‖ Sydrac. [*Cut.*]

Colophon : Imprynted by me Ro-‖bert Wyer : Dwellynge at the ‖ Sygne of S . Iohn̄ Euangelyft ‖ in S . Martyns Paryffhe befyde ‖ Charynge Croffe. [*Name block only.*]

COPY : British Museum (C. 38, a. 8).

REMARKS : This was printed subsequently to the "Troy" book, as it has one of the blocks specially cut for that work. The second tract is a reprint of a part of *The Treatyse perteynynge to Huntynge*, printed by Wynkyn de Worde in 1496.

D

40.—*Boke of Purgatory.* *n.d.* 4to.

DESCRIPTION: [*Title*] Here begynneth a lytell boke, that fpeaketh of purgatorye : and what purgatory is, and of the pains that be therein, and whiche fouls do abyde therein tyll they be purged of synne, and whiche abide not there . And for what fynnes a foul goth to hell, and of the helpe that foules in purgatorie may haue of their friends that be on lyue : and what pardon aueyleth to mannes foule. [*In verse.*]

REFERENCE: Herbert, Vol. 1, p. 384.

41.—*Boke of the xxiiii Stones.* *n.d.* 8vo.

COLLATION: A–B, in eights; 16 ff. ; 27 ll. Type, No. 7.

DESCRIPTION: [*Title*] Here begynneth a lytell bo-‖ke of the xxiiii ftones pryncipalles/ ‖ that profyteth moft to mans body/ as ‖ ye day & the nyght hath xxiiii houres/ ‖ fo be there xxiiii ftones pryncipall. [*Cut.*]

    Colophon : Here endeth the boke of the xxiiii pre-‖cyous ftones pryncipalles . And be for ‖ to fell at the Sygne of feynt Iohñ ‖ Euangelyft/ in feynt Martyns ‖ pariffhe befyde charynge ‖ Croffe. [*Device 2.*]

COPY: British Museum (C. 31, a. 19).

REMARKS: The absence of Wyer's name from the colophon, and the fact that the type in which this was printed is not found in any other of his books, point to this having been printed for him. The type is not unlike some used by Berthelet.

42.—BORDE, ANDREWE. *Dietary of Health. n.d.* 8vo.

COLLATION: A–Q, in fours; 64 ff. ; 24 ll. Types 2, 3, 4 and 5.

DESCRIPTION: [*Title*] Here Folo-‖weth a Compĕdyous Re-‖gyment or a Dyetary of ‖ helth, made in Moũt ‖ pyllor : Compyled ‖ by Andrewe ‖ Boorde, of ‖ Phyficke ‖ Doctor. [*Cut.*]

    Colophon : Imprynted by me Robert ‖ Wyer : Dwellynge at the ‖ fygne of feynt Iohn E-‖uangelyft, in S. Mar-‖tyns Paryffhe, befy-‖de Charynge ‖ Croffe.

COPIES: British Museum (1038, f. 40); Bodleian ; U. L. C.

43.—BOURCHIER, JOHN, *Lord Berners. Castle of Love. n.d.* 8vo.

COLLATION : A–O, in eights ; 112 ff. ; 24 ll. Types 3, 4, 5 and 6.

DESCRIPTION : [*Title*] ¶ The Caſtell of ‖ loue, tranſlated out of Spanyſhe into ‖ Englyſhe, by Iohn̄ Bowrchier ‖ knyght, lorde Bernes, at the in-‖ſtaunce of the Lady Elyzabeth ‖ Carewe, late wyfe to Syr ‖ Nicholas Carewe ‖ knyght . The whiche boke ‖ treateth of the loue be-‖twene Leriano and ‖ Laureola ‖ doughter to the kynge of ‖ Maſedonia. [*Cut.*]

> *Colophon :* Imprynted by ‖ me Robert wyer, ‖ for Richarde ‖ Kele. [*Device No. 2.*]

COPY : British Museum (G. 10332).

REMARKS : The date of printing of this book can be approximated by two circumstances. Sir Nicholas Carew was beheaded in March, 15⅜, and it was probably a year or two after that event. The wood-cut on the title page was one of those used in the *One Hundred Histories of Troy*, so that it was subsequent to the printing of that book.

44.—*Chronicle of the kings of England. n.d.* 8vo.

COLLATION : a–e, in fours ; 20 ff, ; 28 ll. Types 2, 3 and 5.

DESCRIPTION : ¶ Thus endeth the Cronycle and reygne of al the Kyngs that haue ben in Englande & howe longe they reygned, & howe many saints & martyrs haue ben in this land : & ſheweth the hole fūme, from the makyng of the worlde, tyll the commynge of Brute, the which is iiii M lxxvii yeres : & from the c̄omyng of of (*sic.*) Brute to the Incarnaciō of Criſte is a M . C . xxii yeres, & frō the Incarnaciō of Criſte to our Soueraynge lorde kynge, Henry the viii is M v . C . ix yeres . And ſheweth the compaſſe, lengthe, and bredthe of the worlde . : : R .˙. w .˙.

> [d 1.] Here begynneth ‖ the compaſſe, and cyrcuet of the ‖ worlde, and the compaſſe of euery ‖ Ilande cōprehendyd in the fame, and begynneth at the length, ‖ bredeth, and compaſſe of ‖ Englande : with the nombre ‖ of the paryſſhe Churches, Tow-‖nes Byſſhopryckes, and Shyres in ‖ the fame, befyde Cyties and Captelles. [*Cut.*] The prynter ‖ Robert wyer.

D 2

Colophon: ℂ Imprynted by me Robert wyer/ dwel-∥lynge at the fygne of feynt Iohn̄ Euan∥gelyfte/ in feynt Martyns paryffhe ∥ befyde charynge croffe. [*Device 2.*]

COPY: Lambeth Library (imperfect, wanting all before d).

REMARKS: Under the heading of William Marshall, Herbert (p. 500) mentions "An Abridgement of Sebastian Munster's Chronicle, 1542. 8vo.," but without stating the printer, and the author of the article on Marshall in the Dictionary of National Biography, states that this was printed by Robert Wyer, without giving his authority. The earliest edition of Munster's "Cosmography," which seems to be the work referred to, does not appear to have been printed before 1550.

45.—*Declaration of the Chryften Fayth.   n.d.   8vo.*

COLLATION: A–B, in fours; C, six leaves; 14 ff.; 24 ll. Types 2, 4 and 5.

DESCRIPTION: [*Title*] ℂ The declaracyon and power ∥ of the Chryften fayth . [*Cut.*] ℂ He that beleueth on me hath, ∥ euerlaftynge lyfe . Iohn̄ VI.

Colophon: Imprynted by me Robert wyer.

COPY: British Museum (4404, aaa. 26).

46.—*Seven Dialogues.   n.d.   8vo.*

COLLATION: A–C, in fours; D, two leaves; 14 ff.; 24 ll.   Types 2, 3, 4 and 5.

DESCRIPTION: [*Title*] Here be . vii, Dia-∥logues . The fyrft is of the fūne ∥ and of the Moone . The fe-∥conde of Saturne, and of ∥ the Clowde . The . iii . of the ∥ Sterre named Tranf-∥montana, and o-∥ther fterres . ∥ The . iiii . of the euyn Sterre ∥ and the morowe sterre.   The . v . ∥ of the Raynebowe. and the ∥ fygne Cancer . The . vi, ∥ of Heauen, and of ∥ Earth . The . vii ∥ of the Eyre, ∥ and of the ∥ wynde . ∥ ℂ By thefe dialogues, a man ∥ maye take to hym felfe ∥ good Counfayle.

Colophon: Imprynted by me Robert wyer, dwel-∥lynge in feynt Martyns paryffhe . ∥ Ad imprimendum solum.

COPY: British Museum (C. 40, a. 23) ; U. L. C.

47.—*Difference of Astronomy. n.d.* 8vo.

COLLATION : A–E, in fours ; 20 ff. ; 24 ll. Types 3, 4 and 5.

DESCRIPTION : [*Title*] ☊ Here begyn-||neth the dyfference of a-||ſtronomye with the gouer-||nayle to kepe mans body || in helth, all the foure || seasons of the || yeare. [*Cut.*]

> *Colophon :* Imprynted by || me Robert wyer || Dwellynge at the Sygne || of Seynt Iohn̄ Euan-||gelyſt in Seynt Mar-||tyns Paryſſhe befyde || Charynge || Croſſe. [*Device No. 2.*]

COPIES : British Museum (C. 40, a. 21) ; Another copy (7383, aa. 2).

48.—*Diurnal. n.d.* 8vo.

COLLATION : A–C², in fours.

DESCRIPTION : [*Title*] A dyurnall for deuoute soules : to ordre theym selfe therafter. [*Woodcut.*]

> *Colophon :* Imprynted by me Robert wyer dwellynge at the sygne of saynt Iohan Euangelyst, in saynt Martyns parysshe besyde charynge crosse. Cum priuilegio Regali : pro spatio septem annorum. [Verso of last leaf, *Device 2*, and the words, "These be for to sell, at the synge of seynt Iohn̄ Euangelyste."]

COPY : Private Library.

49.—*Dreams of Daniel. n.d.* 8vo.

COLLATION : A–F, in fours ; 24 ff.

DESCRIPTION : [*Title*] Here begynneth the Dreames of Daniell . With the Exposycions of the XII . Sygnes, deuyded by the . XII . monthes of the yeare . And also the Destenys both of man and woman borne in eche monthe of the yere . Very necessarye to be knowen. [*Cut.*]

REFERENCE : Dibdin, Vol. 3, p. 202.

NOTE : The *Interpretation of Dreams* occupies 3 ll. ; the *Expositions,* 5 ll. ; the *Destenys,* 15 ll.

50.—ERASMUS (DESIDERIUS). *Epistle on the Sacrament. n.d.* 8vo.

COLLATION: A–D, in fours; 16 ff.; 23 ll. Types 2, 3, 4, 5 and 6.

DESCRIPTION: [*Title*] ¶ An Epiſtle of || the famous clerke Eraſmus || of Roterodame, concernynge the || veryte of the Sacrament of Chriſtes || body and bloude, whiche Epiſtle is || ſet before the excellent boke, inti-||tuled D. Algeri De veritate cor-||poris et ſanguinis dominici in || Euchariſtia. which boke was || made by the ſayd Algerus || aboute fyue hondred || yeares paſſed . || And nowe of late yeares, hath agayne || ben ouerſeen and reuyſyted, by the || ſayde famous clerke Eraſmus || of Roterodame, and de-||dycated by hym, || vnto the Reuerende father || Balthaſar byſſhop || of Hyldeſyn . || ¶ Thys preſent Epistle of Eraſmus makynge || is to be founde oute, in the great volume of || all his Epiſtles, pagina 1577, Hauynge || this lytell wrytynge ouer it, || In Algerum.

Colophon: Imprynted by me Robert wyer.

COPY: British Museum (3925, b. 17).

51.—ERASMUS, D. *Governance of good helthe. n.d.* 8vo.

COLLATION: A–D, in fours; 16 ff.; 27 ll. Types 2, 3, 4, 5 and 6.

DESCRIPTION: [*Title*] ¶ The gouernaũ-||ce of good helthe, by the moſte || excellent phyloſopher Plutarche, || the moſte eloquent Eraſmus || beynge interpretoure . [*Cut.*] Thou wylte repent that this || came not ſooner to thy hand.

Colophon: ¶ Imprynted by me Robert Wyer.

COPIES: British Museum (1039, a. 6); Huth Library.

52.—ERASMUS, D. *Governance of good helthe. n.d.* 8vo.

COLLATION: A–D, in fours; 16 ff.; 27 ll.

DESCRIPTION: [*Title*] ¶ The gouernaũ-||ce of good helthe, by the moſte || excellent phyloſopher Plutarche, || the moſte eloquent Eraſmus || beynge interpretoure . || [*Cut.*] ¶ Thou wylte repent that this || came not ſooner to thy hande .

Colophon : ⚏ Imprynted by me Robert ‖ Wyer . ‖ ⚏ Cum priuilegio regali ad im-‖primendum folum . ‖

COPY : University Library, Cambridge.

53.—*Estate of the Comonalty.* *n.d.* 8vo.

COLLATION : A–K, in fours.

DESCRIPTION : [*Title*] Here begynneth a lytell neceffary Treatyfe the whiche fpeketh of the eftate of Comonalte, and of the people, and howe they ought to gouern them in good maners. [*Device No. 3.*]

    Colophon : Imprinted by me ——— in feynt Martyns paryffhe befyde Charynge Croffe. [*Device No. 2.*]

COPY : Spencer Collection.
REFERENCE : Herbert, Vol. I, p. 383.

54.—*Examples howe mortall synne.* *n.d.* 8vo.

COLLATION : A–I, in fours ; 36 ff.

DESCRIPTION : [*Title*] Examples ‖ howe mortall synne maketh ‖ the synners inobedyentes ‖ to have many paynes and ‖ doloures within the ‖ fyre of Hell . ‖ And fyrft Example of a Fa-‖ther of an houfeholde the ‖ whiche saw two pon-‖des and the tourmen-‖tes of Hell. [*Cut.*]

    Colophon : Imprynted by me Robert Wyer in Seynt Martyns Paryffhe, befyde Charynge Croffe.

COPY : Bodleian (Douce H. 47).

55.—*Foundement of contemplacyon.* *n.d.* 8vo.

COLLATION : A, eight leaves ; B, four leaves.

DESCRIPTION : [*Title*] ⚏ The Foundement of contemplacyon . How a man shall contemple, and fe God in creatures . The Fyrfte chapytre. [*Device No. 3.*]

    Colophon : Imprynted by me ——— in faynt Martyns paryffhe . Cum priuilegio regali.

REFERENCE : Herbert, Vol. I, p. 382.
REMARKS : A reprint of the *Shorte treatise of contemplatyon*, printed by Wynkyn de Worde.

56.—*The Four Tokens.*   *n.d.*   8vo.

COLLATION : A–B, in fours ; 8 ff. ; 19 ll.   Types 3 and 4.

DESCRIPTION : [*Title*] ⓠ As Iheroni-∥mus, fheweth . In this ∥ begynnynge, so wyll ∥ I wryte of the iiii ∥ Tokens, the ∥ whiche ∥ fhall be fhewed afore ∥ the dredeful·daye ∥ of Dome, of ∥ our lorde ∥ Ihefu Chrifte . For ∥ there fhall we ∥ fhewe ourfelf ∥ yonge and ∥ olde, etc . ∥ ✠

> *Colophon :* ⓠ This tranflated out of ∥ Duche into Englyffhe ∥ by Iohñ Doufbrugh . ∥ Imprinted by me ∥ Robert Wyer.   [*Device No. 2.*]

COPY : British Museum (4856, a.)

57.—GODFRIDUS.   *Book of Aftronomye.*   *n.d.*   8vo.

COLLATION : A–K, in fours ; 40 ff. ; 23 ll.   Types 2, 3, 4, 5 and 8.

DESCRIPTION : [*Title*] Here begyn-∥neth the Boke of know-∥ledge of thynges unknowen ap-∥perteyninge to Astronomye ∥ with certayne neceffarye ∥ Rules, and certayne spe-∥res contaynyng herein . Compyled by Godfri-∥dus super Palla-∥dium de Agricul-∥tura Angli-∥catum.

> *Colophon :* Imprynted by me Robert Wyer Dwellynge at the fygne of S . Iohñ Euangelyft, in S . Martyns Paryffhe befyde Charynge Crofle.

COPIES : British Museum (C. 27, a. 38) ; Bodleian.

58.—GOODALE, IOHN.   *A Ciuile Nofgay.*   *n.d.* [c. 1550].   8vo.

COLLATION : A–E⁴, in eights ; 36 ff. ; 25 and 22 ll.   Types 2, 3, 4, 5 and 6.

DESCRIPTION : [*Title*] ⓠ A ciuile Nof-∥gay wherein is contayned ∥ not onelye the office and ∥ dewty of all mageftrates ∥ and Iudges but alfo of ∥ of all fubjectes with a ∥ preface concernynge ∥ the lyberty of Iu-∥ftice in this our ∥ tyme newly ∥ collec-∥ted and gethered out of ∥ Latyn and fo tranfla-∥ted in to the Ing-∥lyfhe tonge by ∥ I . G . [F. 1ᵇ, Preface ; 6ᵃ, Contents ; 6ᵇ, *Device No. 3.*]

> *Colophon :* [35ᵇ] ⓠ Imprynted ∥ by me Robart wyer ∥ for Ihon ∥ goodale . ∥ [F. 36, *wanting.*]

COPIES : British Museum (3905, a. 34) ; Lambeth.

REMARKS : The following events noted in this book, fix the date of its printing :—The destruction of Papal authority (1534) ; Capture of Boulogne (1544) ; Sundry overthrow of Scots (1547). Its probable date was about 1550.

59.—GOODALE, IOHN. *Lyberties of the Cleargy.* n.d. 8vo.

COLLATION : A–D, in fours ; 16 ff. ; 24 ll. Types 3, 4 and 5.

DESCRIPTION : [*Title*] ❡ The Lyberties || of the Cleargy Collected out || of the Lawes of this Realme || both necessary for Vycars || and Curates . Com-||pyled by Iohn Goodale. [*Device No. 3.*]

> *Colophon :* [Verso of D⁴] Imprynted by me Robert Wyer.

COPIES : British Museum (C. 12, c. 25) ; Lambeth Library.

60.—GOODWYN, CHRISTOPHER. *Maydens dreme.* n.d. [c. 1542]. 4to.

COLLATION : A–B, in fours ; 8 ff.

DESCRIPTION : [*Title*] The Maydens Dreme! Compyled and made by Christofer Goodwyn . In the yere of our Lorde M CCCCC xlij. [*Cut.*]

> *Colophon :* Imprynted by me Robert wyer for Richard Bankes. Cum priuilegio Regali. [*Device No. 2.*]

REFERENCES : Dibdin, Vol. 3, pp. 208, 209 ; Collier's *Bibl. Account of Rare Books,* Vol. 1, pp. 317, 318.

61.—GUIDO DE CAULIACO. *Questionary of Surgeons* [1542]. 4to.

COLLATION : A–Y, in fours ; A–H, in fours ; 30 ll. Types 2, 3, 4, 5 and 6.

DESCRIPTION : [*Title*] ❡ The queſtyonary of || Cyrurgyens, with the formulary of || lytell Guydo in Cyrurgie, with || the ſpectacles of Cyrurgyens || newly added, with the || fourth Boke of the || Terapentyke [*sic*], or Methode curatyfe of || Claude Galyen prynce of Phyſyciens, || with a Synguler treaty of the cure || of vlceres, newely Enprynted at || London, by me Robert wyer, || And be for to ſell in Poules || Churcheyarde, at the || ſygne of Iudyth . || Cum priuilegio ad impri-||mendum ſolum . || Iudyth. [*Cut and two border pieces.*]

> *Colophon :* ❡ Imprynted by me Robert wyer for Henry Dabbe! & Rycharde Banckes . Cum pri||uilegio regali ad imprimendū ſolum || per ſeptiennium [*sic*] annum.

COPIES : British Museum (549, b. 24, 1) ; Huth Library ; Trinity College, Cambridge.

REMARKS : There seems to be some error about the date assigned to this book. On A, 1 it is stated that Robert Copland finished the translation of the *Fourth boke* on the iiij day of February M . CCCCC xlij. As the years began and ended in March at that time, this book was more probably printed in 1543.

62.—Heywood, Iohn. *Play of the wether.* *n.d.* 4to.
Reference: Dibdin, Vol. 3, p. 189.

63.—Hilton, Walter. *The Medled Lyfe.* *n.d.* [c. 1531]. 8vo.
Collation: a–f, in fours; 24 ff.; 28 ll. Types 2 and 3.

Description: [*Title*] Here begyñeth the Medled lyfe ‖ Compyled by
mayſter watre Hylton,' to a ‖ devoute man in temperall Eſtate/ howe ‖ he
ſhulde rule hym/ whiche is right ex-‖pedyent for euery man/ and moſte
in ‖ eſpecyall for them that lyue in the ‖ Medled lyfe/ And it ſheweth
what Medled lyfe is. [*Cuts.*] [F, 24ᵇ] ℭ Thus endeth this lytell
treatyſe intytuled ‖ the Medled lyfe compyled by Walter Hyl‖ton/ at the
inſtaūce of a deuoute man of ‖ temporall eſtate.

   Colophon : Imprynted by me ‖ Robert wyre/ dwellynge at the ‖
Sygne of Saynt Iohñ Euage-‖lyſt : in ſaynt Martyns paryſ-‖ſhe/ beſyde
Charynge croſſe.

Copy: Bodleian (Mason, C. C. 52*).

Remarks: The spelling of the printer's name in the colophon is the same as in No. 1,
   dated 1531.

64.—Hogarde, Myles (?). *Treatyſe in three Parts.* *n.d.* 4to.
Collation: Λ–I, in fours; 36 ff.; 32 ll. [*In verse.*] Types 2, 3, 4 and 5.

Description : [*Title*] ℭ Here begyñeth a newe ‖ Treatyſe deuyded in thre
partyes, ‖ the fyrst parte is to know, and haue ī mynde ‖ the wretchednes,
of all mankynde . ‖ The ſeconde is of the cōdycion and manere ‖ Of the
unſtedfaſtnes, of this world here . ‖ The thyrde parte ī this boke you may
rede ‖ Of bytter death, and why it is to drede . [*Cuts.*] The myght of the
Father almyghty, ‖ The wyt of the Sone all wytty ‖ And the goodnes of
the holy Ghoſte ‖ God and Lorde of mightes moſte ‖ Be our helpe,' and
our ſpede ‖ Nowe and euer in all our nede ‖ and ſpecyally at this
begynnynge ‖ And brynge vs all to good endynge . ‖ Amen.

   Colophon : ℭ Imprynted by me ‖ Robert wyer,' dwel-‖lynge in ſaynt
Martyns pa-‖ryſſhe/ at the ſygne of ſaynt ‖ Iohñ Euangelyſt/ be‖ſyde
Charynge ‖ Croſſe . ‖ Ad imprimendum ſolum. [*Device No. 2.*]

Copy : British Museum (C. 40, c. 11).

65.—HOGARDE, MYLES.—*A New Treatise in manner of a Dialogue.* *n.d.* [c. 1550]. 4to.

COLLATION: A–D, in fours; 16 ff.; [*In verse*]. Types 3, 4, 5 and 6.

DESCRIPTION: [*Title*] A new treatyfe in ma-||ner of a Dialoge' which fheweth the || excellency of mañes nature/ in that || he is made to the Image of God, || and wherein it reftyth/ and by || howe many wayes a man || dothe blotte and defyle || the fame Image . [*Cut.*] Remembre man, thou art earth playne, || And thereto fhalt, return agayne . Job . [Poem begins on title page.]

> *Colophon*: Imprynted by me || Robert wyer' dwellinge in S . || Martins paryfhe at Cha-||rynge Croffe . || Ad imprimendum folum.

COPY: British Museum (C. 40, c. 14).

REMARKS: The author, Miles Hogarde, was fervant to Queen Mary, and the author of feveral pieces between 1550 and 1555. As it ends with the words "God save the King," it must have been written either in the reign of Henry the eighth or his son.

66.—HORAE. [1535?] 12mo.

COLLATION: 120 ff. and prefatory matter.

DESCRIPTION: [*Title*] Hore beate virginis Marie (ad ufum facro fancte ecclefie Sarum) iam fequuntur.

> *Colophon:* Robertus wyer me excudebat, in parochio diui Martini, moram trahenti fub interfigno fancti Ioannis. [*Device No. 3.*]

REFERENCE: Herbert's edition of *Ames' Typ. Antiq.*, Vol. 1, p. 371. There is no indication of the character of the types. The date is determined by the Calendar.

67.—HUNNIS, WILLIAM. *Abridgement of the Psalms.* *n.d.* 8vo.

DESCRIPTION: [*Title*] Abridgement or brief meditation on certain of the Psalms in English meeter.

REFERENCES: Herbert, Vol. 1, p. 377; *Warton's Hist. of Eng. Poet.*, Hazlitt's edition, Vol. 4, p. 139.

68.—*Judgement of Urines.*   *n.d.*   8vo.

COLLATION : A–I, in fours ; 36 ff. ; 24 ll.   Types 3, 4 and 5.

DESCRIPTION : [*Title*] Hereafter ‖ foloweth the Iudgemēt ‖ of all Urynes :
And for ‖ to knowe the mañes ‖ from the womannes′ and ‖ beaſtes both
from the ‖ mañes & womans′ ‖ with the coloure ‖ of euerye ‖ Vryne . ‖
Exercyſed & Practyſed ‖ with dyuerſe other ‖ by Doctor Smyth ‖ and other
at ‖ Mountpyller. ‖ [*Cut.*]

    Colophon : Here endeth ‖ the boke of ſeyng of waters . ‖ Imprynted
by me Robert ‖ Wyer : Dwellynge at the ‖ Sygne of ſeynt Iohñ Euan-‖gelyſt,
in ſeynt Martyns ‖ Paryſſhe beſyde Cha-‖rynge Croſſe.   [*Device No. 2.*]

COPY : British Museum (1189, a. 38).

69.—LARKE, IOHN.   *Book of Noblenes.*   *n.d.*   8vo.

COLLATION : A–H, in eights ; 64 ff.   Leaf 64 not known.

DESCRIPTION : [*Title*] &c., The Bo‖ke of No-‖blenes . ‖ That ſheweth how
ma-‖ny ſortes & kyndes there is.   And ſpecially ‖ to thoſe whiche do
folowe & vſe the ‖ trayne and eſtate of warre, tranſla-‖ted out of laten
into Frenche, ‖ and now into Engliſſhe, ‖ by me Iohñ ‖ Larke.   [*Cut.*]

COPY : University Library, Cambridge (Herbert's copy).

REFERENCE : Herbert, Vol. 1, p. 380.

REMARKS : Perhaps this is an edition of the same book as that described briefly as *The
Ordere & Trayne of War*, printed by Wyer for John Gough.

70.—*Letter from the Holy Ghost.*   *n.d.*   4to.

COLLATION : A, six leaves ; 31 ll.   Types 3 and 5.

DESCRIPTION : [*Title*] ℂ A lettre frō the holy ‖ ghost : to preeſtes and ‖
religious perſones′ ‖ conceyued by yma-‖ginacyon . ‖ ℂ With a lettre frō
the ‖ Father and ſone ‖ and holy ghost : ‖ dyrected to ‖ all men . ‖ ℂ And
after foloweth ‖ the thre verytes . ‖ ✠

    Colophon : Imprynted by me ‖ Robert Wyer/ for Rychard bankes ‖
Cum Privilegio Regali.   [*Device No. 2.*]

COPY : Ch. Ch. Coll. Oxford (Polygraphy, f. 27, 3).

71.—LITTLETON, SIR THOMAS. *Tenures. n.d.* 24mo.

COLLATION : 256 leaves.

DESCRIPTION : [*Title*] Littletons Tenures in English.

REFERENCE : Herbert, Vol. 1, p. 376.

72.—MACER, ÆMILIUS. *Herball. n.d.* 8vo,

COLLATION : A–P, in fours ; 27 ll.   Types 2, 3, and 5.

DESCRIPTION : [*Title*] ☾ A newe Her-||ball of Macer, || Tranſlated || out of La-||ten in to || Englyſſhe.

> *Colophon :* ☾ Imprynted by || me Robert wyer, || dwellynge in ſaint Martyns pa-||ryſhe, at the ſygne of ſaynt || Iohn̄ Euangelyſt, || beſyde Charyn||ge Croſſe . || ✠ .

COPY : British Museum (7509, a).

73.—MACER ÆMILIUS. *Herbal. n.d.* 8vo.

COLLATION : A–W, in fours ; 24 ll.   Types 2, 3, 4, 5 and 8.

DESCRIPTION : [*Title*] Macers || Herbal || Practy-||ſyd by || Doctor || Lynacro || Translated out of laten, || into Englyſſhe, whiche || ſhewynge theyr Ope-||racyons & Vertues, || ſet in the margent || of this Boke, to || the extent you || myght knowe || theyr Ver-||tues.

> *Colophon :* Imprynted by || me Robert wyer || dwellynge in ſeynt Martyns Pa-||ryſſhe at the ſygne of ſeynt || Iohn̄ Euangelyſt, beſyde Charyn-||ge Croſſe.   [*Device No. 2.*]

COPY : British Museum (546, b. 26).

REMARKS : This is proved to be a later edition than the one printed in secretary, by having an addition to the list of herbs under (A.).

74.—*Maydens Crosse Rewe. n.d.* 4to.

COLLATION : 4 leaves.

DESCRIPTION : [*Title*] Here is a necessarye Treatyse for all maner of persons to reade, and hath to name the Mayden's Croſſe Rewe.

REFERENCES : Dibdin, Vol. 3, p. 208 ; Collier, *Bibl. Account,* Vol. 1, p. 509.

NOTE : A poetical tract of 30 seven-line stanzas.   At the end " Finis q-d Robert Wyer."

75.—Moulton, Thomas. *Glaſſe of Helth. n.d.* 8vo.

Collation: a–i, in fours; 36 ff.; 28 ll. Types 2, 3 and 4.

Description : [*Title*] This is the glaſſe ‖ of Helth, a great Treaſure ‖ for pore men/ neceſſary and nedefull for ‖ euery perſon to loke in/ that wyll kepe ‖ theyr body from sycneſſes and dyſſeaſes . ‖ And it ſheweth howe the Planet-‖tes reygne euery houre of the ‖ daye & the nyght/ with the ‖ Natures & expoſycyons ‖ of yᵉ xii Sygnes/ deuy‖ded by the xii mon-‖thes of the yere/ ‖ And after foloweth of all yᵉ euyll and daunge-‖rous dayes of the yere . And ſheweth the ‖ remedyes/ for dyuers Infyrmytyes & ‖ dyſeaſes, yᵗ hurteth the body of man . ‖ [*Cut.*] ⊄ Theſe ben the iii . ‖ peryllous ‖ Mōdayes ‖ in the yere ‖ to let blod ‖ or to take ‖ any medy-‖cyn or pur-‖gacion on, ‖ that is for ‖ to ſayne/ ‖ The fyrſte ‖ Mondaye ‖ of Auguſt ‖ And yᵉ ſecū‖de is yᵉ laſt ‖ Mōday of ‖ Apryll . And the thyrde is the laſtt Mondaye ‖ of Decembre.

     Colophon : Imprynted by me Robert wyer, dwellyn-‖ge at the ſygne of ſaynt Iohñ Euange-‖lyſt in ſaynt Martyns paryſſh beſyde ‖ Charynge Croſſe.

Copy: British Museum (C. 31, a. 29).

Remarks: This was probably the earliest of the three editions printed by Wyer, strokes being used largely for punctuation.

76.—Moulton, Thomas. *Glaſſe of Helth. n.d.* 8vo.

Collation: a–i, in fours; 36 ff.; 28 ll. Types 2, 3 and 4.

Description : [*Title*] This is the glaſſe ‖ of Helthe : A great Treaſure ‖ for poore men, neceſſary and nedeful for ‖ euery perſon to loke in, that wyll kepe ‖ theyr body from ſyckeneſſes and dyſ-‖ſeaſes . And it ſheweth howe the ‖ Planettes reygne euery houre ‖ of the daye and the nyght, ‖ with the Natures and expoſicions of ‖ the . xii . Sygnes . deuyded by the . ‖ xii . Monthes of the yeare . ‖ And after foloweth of all the euyll and daun‖gerous dayes of the yere . And ſheweth the ‖ remedyes for dyuers

Infyrmyties and ‖ dyſſeaſes yᵗ hurteth the body of man . ‖ [*Cut.*]
⊄ Theſe ‖ ben the . iii . ‖ peryllous ‖ Mōdayes ‖ in the yere ‖ to let
blode ‖ or to take ‖ any medy‖cine or pur‖gacion on ‖ that is for ‖ to
fayne . ‖ The fyrſte ‖ Mondaye ‖ of Auguſt ‖ And the ſe‖cōde is the ‖
laſte Mon‖daye of Apryll . And the thyrde is the laſte ‖ Mondaye of
Decembre.

    Colophon : ⊄ Imprynted by me Robert ‖ wyer, dwellynge in
faynt ‖ Martyns paryſſhe, at ‖ charynge Croſſe . ‖ Ad imprimendum
folum. [*Device No. 2.*]

COPY : British Museum (C. 31, a. 24).

REMARKS : This was another edition with slight variations of spelling. Strokes were not
   used in this for punctuation until the last two leaves were in the press, when the stock
   of commas ran out.

77.—MOULTON, THOMAS. *Myrrour or Glaſſe of Helth.* *n.d.* 8vo.

COLLATION : A–G, in eights ; H, five leaves ; 61 ff. ; 23 ll. Types 3, 4
   and 5.

DESCRIPTION : [*Title*] This is the ‖ Myrrour or Glaſſe of Helth ‖ neceſſary
   and nedefull for euery per-; ſon to loke in that will kepe their bo-‖dye from
   the fyckneſſe of the Peſti-‖lence, and it ſheweth how the planet-‖tes do
   raygne in euery houre of the ‖ day and nyghte, with the na-‖tures and
   expoſiciōs of the XII ‖ fygnes deuyded by ‖ the XII Monethes ‖ of the yeare,
   and ‖ ſhewed the ‖ reme-‖dies for many dyuers infirmities ‖ and dyſeaſes
   that hurteth ‖ the bodye of ‖ Manne.

    Colophon : Imprynted by ‖ me Robert wyer ‖ Dwellynge at the
Sygne ‖ of Seynt Iohñ Euan-‖gelyst, in Seynt Mar-‖tyns Paryſſhe befyde ‖
Charynge ‖ Croſſe . ‖ ✠ [*Device No. 2.*]

COPY : British Museum (C. 31, c. 16).

REMARKS : This has the Pestilence part put first, and frequent mention is made of the
   " plague nowe raging." Plague was rife in London in 1543, 1546 and 1552, to any
   of which years the book may belong.

78.—*New Idol and Old Devil.* n.d. 8vo.

COLLATION : a–e, in eights ; 40 ff. ; 23 ll.

DESCRIPTION : [*Title*] A Boke made ‖ by a certayne ‖ great clerke, agaynſt the ‖ newe Idole and olde ‖ Deuyll/ whiche of ‖ late tyme, in Miſ‖nia ſhulde haue ‖ ben canony‖ſed for a ‖ faynt. [Verso of title page, *Device No. 3.*]

Colophon : Imprynted by ‖ me Robert Wyer dwel-‖lynge in faynt Mar-‖tyns paryſſhe, be‖ſyde charynge ‖ Crosse ℂ Cum priuilegio. [*Device No. 2.*]

NOTE : Dibdin placed this among the dated books under 1534, but this was the date of the translation and first printing in England, not necessarily the date at which Wyer printed it, though the type and general appearance of the book is not against the supposition.

79.—*Ordinal or Statute concerning Artyficers.* n.d. 8vo.

COLLATION : A–E, in eights ; 40 ff. ; 22 ll. Types 3 and 5.

DESCRIPTION : [*Title*] The Ordynal ‖ or Statutȝ concernynge Arty-‖fycers, feruauntes, & labou-‖rers/ newly prynted ‖ with dyuers other ‖ thyngȝ thereunto ‖ added. [*Device No. 3.*]

Colophon : Imprynted by me Robert ‖ wyer/ for Rycharde ‖ Bankes . ‖ Cum priuilegio regali/ ‖ ad imprimendum folum.

COPY : British Museum ($\frac{129.4.3}{3}$).

REMARKS : In this a Statute of 33, Hen. 8th (1541–1542) is quoted. Probably printed 1542 or 1543.

80.—*Ordre or Trayne of Warre.* n.d. 8vo.

COLLATION : Not given.

DESCRIPTION : [*Title*] Here followeth the ordre or Trayne of Warre, that a prynce or heed Captayne ought to take . etc.

Colophon : Imprynted by me ——— in Seynt Martyns pariſſhe at Charynge Croſſe Imprynted for Iohn Gowgh. Cum priuilegio Regali ad imprimendum folum. [*Device No. 3.*]

REFERENCE : Herbert, Vol. 1, p. 384.

81.—*Our ladyes Chambre/ or Parler.* *n.d.* 12mo.

COLLATION : a, eight leaves ; b, six leaves.

REFERENCE : Herbert, Vol. I. p. 383.

82.—PANTOLABUS, PONCE. *Genealogye of Heresy.* *n.d.* s. sh.

DESCRIPTION : [*Title*] The Genealogye of herefye . Compyled by Ponce
Pantolabus.

  Colophon : Imprented by me Robert Wyer . Ad imprimendum folum.

REFERENCE : Herbert, Vol. I, pp. 373, 374.

REMARKS : This was assailed (and the text quoted) by John Bale in his *Mystery of Iniquity*,
printed at Geneva (?) in 1545, but dated 1542.

83.—*Perfyte Pronoftycacion.* *n.d.* 4to.

COLLATION : A–C, in fours ; 12 ff. Types 2, 3, 4, 5 and 6.

DESCRIPTION : [*Title*] A Perfyte ‖ Pronoftycacion perpetuall ‖ Very easy to
be vnderftande, of ‖ the Reader . Yea and alfo for them ‖ whiche knoweth
not a letter on ‖ the Booke . And it is good for ‖ Husbandmen of the
Coun-‖trey, to knowe and vnder-‖ftande the yeares, that ‖ fhall be
plenteous ‖ and in great ha-‖bundaûce of ‖ Goodes . ‖ And the yeres the
whiche ‖ fhall be greuous, and in ‖ fcafytie with other fygnes ‖ conteyned
herein, as ‖ appereth in this Booke.

  Colophon : Impryn‖ted by me Robert wyer : ‖ dwellynge at the Sygne
of ‖ S . Iohn Euägelyft befyde ‖ Charynge Croffe. [*Device No. 2.*]

COPY : British Museum (717. a. 46).

REMARKS : This was probably printed by a workman in the office. The illustrations might
have been cut by a schoolboy with a blunt knife. The almanac begins in 1556.

84.—PRACTICA PLUTARCHE. *n.d.* 8vo.

COLLATION : A, six leaves ; 22 and 23 ll. Types 2, 3, 4, 5 and 8.

DESCRIPTION : [*Title*] Practica Plu-‖tarche the ex-‖cellent Phy-‖lofopher. [*Cut.*]

  Colophon : Imprynted by me Robert wyer.

COPY : British Museum (C. 31. a.).

85.—PROCLUS, DIADOCHUS. *Description of the World.* *n.d.* 8vo.

COLLATION : A–F, in fours ; 24 ff. ; 23 ll.   Types 2, 3, 4, 5 and 6.

DESCRIPTION : [*Title*] ⊄ The Descripci-||on of the Sphere || or Frame of || the worlde.   [*Cut.*]

  Colophon : Imprynted by me Ro-||bert Wyer : Dwellynge at the || Sygne of S . Iohn̄ Euangelyſt/ || in S . Martyns Paryſſhe beſyde Charynge Croſſe . || Cum priuilegio, Ad || imprimendum ſolum.

COPY : British Museum (717, a. 50).

86.—*Prognostication of Erra Pater.* *n.d.* 8vo.

COLLATION : a–c, in fours ; 12 ff. ; 28 ll.   Types 2, 3 and 5.

DESCRIPTION : [*Title*] The Pronoſty-||cacyon for euer, of Mayſter Erra || Pater Aſtronomyer, the whiche Pro-||noſtyke vpon the . iiii . maner of Coo-||les, that come of the . iiii . Complexi-||ons . And ſheweth the foure Sea||ſons of the yere, vpon the . xii . || Monethes of blode lettyng, || with the Dyſpoſycyon of || the dayes of the moone : || after her Influence, ∥ and Ariſtotilis de || aſtronomiis af-||ſyrmeth the || ſame.   [*Cut.*]

  Colophon : Imprynted by me Robert wyer, dwel||lynge at the sygne of ſaynt Iohn̄ || Eũangelyſt, in ſaynt Martyns || paryſſhe, beſyde Cha-||rynge Croſſe : || Cum priuilegio Regali.   [*Device No. 2.*]

COPY : British Museum (234, a. 28).

87.—*Prognostication.* *n.d.* 8vo.

COLLATION : A–D, in fours ; 16 ff. ; 24 ll.   Types 5, 6 and 8.

DESCRIPTION : [*Title*] PROGNO-||STICACION Dra-||wen out of the Bookes of || Ipocras, Auicen, and other no-||table Auctours of Phyſycke, || ſhewynge the daunger of || dyuers ſyckeneſſes, that || is to ſay, whether peryll || of death be in them || or not, the pleaſure || of almyghtye || God refer-||ued. [*Cut.*]   The Prognoſty-||cacion/ of diſeaſes.

  Dᵗ *recto :* ⊄ Finis q₈ . R . W . ||

  Colophon : Imprynted by me || Robert Wyer . || Cum priuilegio ad impri-||mendum ſolum.   [*Device No. 2.*]

COPY : British Museum (1038, c. 5. 2).

88.—*Prognostication.* *n.d.* 12mo.

DESCRIPTION: [*Title*] Pronosticum Magiſtri Gasparis Laet de Borchlaen medicine doctoris, ad meridianum insignis emporii Antwerpiensis/ pro Anno Domini M . CCCCC . xxx compilatum et practicum.

    Colophon : These be for to sell at the Sygne of Seynt Iohñ Euangelyst/ in seynt Martyns parysshe besyde Charynge Crosse.

COPY: British Museum, *Bagford Papers*, a fragment.

89.—*School House of Women.* *n.d.* 8vo.

COLLATION: Not given.

DESCRIPTION: [*Title*] Here begynneth a lytell boke named the ſcole howſe, wherein euery man may rede a goodly prayſe of the condycyons of women.

    Colophon : (Within a border), Robert Wyer the printer.

REFERENCE: Herbert, Vol. 1, p. 375.

90.—*Seeing of Urines.* *n.d.* 8vo.

COLLATION: A–H, in fours; 32 ff.; 28 ll. Types 2, 3, 4, and 5.

DESCRIPTION: [*Title*] Here begynneth || the feyng of Urynes, of all || the coloures that Ury-||nes be of/ And the || Medycynes an-||nexed to eue-||ry Uryne : || very neceſſary for || euery man to || knowe. [*Cut.*]

    Colophon : Imprynted by me Robert || wyer/ || dwellynge at the fyg-||ne of faynt Iohñ Euan-||gelyſt in faynt Mar-||tyns paryſſhe. [*Device No. 2, without the name block.*]

COPY: British Museum (7461, a).

91.—STANBRIDGE, I. *Vocabula.* *n.d.* 4to.

COLLATION: A–E, in fours; F, two leaves; 22 ff.; Types 2, 3, 4 and 5.

DESCRIPTION: [*Title*] Vocabula magiſtri || ſtãbrigii ſua ſaltũ || editione edita.

    Colophon : Imprynted by me Ro||bert wyer, dwellynge at || the fygne of faynt Io-||han Euangelyſte/ || in faynt martyns || paryſſhe/ befyde || Charynge || Croſſe. [*Device No. 2.*]

COPY: Bodleian (Tanner, 239).

92.—*Ten Places of Scripture. n.d.* 8vo.

COLLATION : b–f, in fours, besides title and following leaf ; 22 ff.

DESCRIPTION : [*Title*] Hereafter folowe x certayne Places of Scrypture, by whom it is proved, that the doctrynes and tradycons of men ought to be auoyded.

Colophon : Imprynted by me Robert Wyer dwellynge in Saynt Martyns paryſſhe beſyde Charynge Croſſe . Cum priuilegio.

REFERENCES : A copy sold at Sotheby's, June 30th, 1885, No. 1055 ; Hazlitt's Coll. and Notes, 3rd Series, p. 226 ; Herbert, Vol. 1, p. 378 ; Maunsell's Catalogue, p. 32.

93.—*Three Practyses. n.d.* 16mo.

DESCRIPTION : [*Title*] Here foloweth three Practyses, nowe used at Mount pyller by monsyre Emery a Romayne borne in Rome.

REFERENCE : Hazlitt's Handbook, p. 184.

94.—*Treatise answering the Book of Berdes. n.d.* 4to.

COLLATION : A–B, in fours ; 8 ff. ; 26 ll. Types 3 and 4.

DESCRIPTION : [*Title*] ⊄ The treatyſe anſwe-||rynge the boke of || Berdes . || Compyled by Collyn Clowte dedy-||cated to Barnarde barber || dwellynge in Banbery. [*Cuts.*]

Colophon : [Verso of B, 4] Barnes in the de-||fence of the Berde. [*Device No. 3*] Seven lines of verse, with initials R . W . [? Robert Wyer] & privilege.

COPY : British Museum (C. 40, e. 6).

REMARKS : This was a satire upon Andrew Borde's *Book of Berdes*, now lost. In the Preface, the author refers to another of Borde's publications, the *Introductorye to Knowlege*, printed in 1547 by Will. Middleton.

95.—*Treatyſe of Good Works. n.d.* 8vo.

COLLATION : A–T, in eights (part of A missing) ; V, six leaves ; 23 ll. Types 2, 3 and 5.

DESCRIPTION : [*Title*] Here after en-‖ſueth a propre ‖ treatyse of ‖ good ‖ workes . ‖ ☙

    Colophon : Imprynted by me Robert ‖ Wyer dwel-‖lynge in ‖ faynt martyns ‖ paryſſhe beſy-‖de charynge ‖ Croſſe . ‖ ℂ Cum priuilcgio. [*Device No. 2.*]

COPY : St. John's College, Oxford.

REMARKS : The type in this is clear and the blocks in a good state. It was probably printed about the same time as the *Exhortations of Erasmus* [q. v.].

96.—VAUGHAN, ROBERT. *Dyalogue ... for women.* *n.d.* [c. 1542]. 4to.

COLLATION : Not given.

DESCRIPTION : [*Title*] A dyalogue defensyue for women/ agaynſt malycyous detractours.

    Colophon : Thus endeth the faucon and the Pye . Anno dñi 1542 . Imprynted by me Robert Wyer, for Richard Banckes . Cum priuilegio regali, ad imprimendū solū, per septem annum. [*Device No. 2.*]

REFERENCE : Dibdin, Vol. 3, p. 181.

97.—VIGO, IOANNES DE. *Lytell Practyce.* *n.d.* 8vo.

COLLATION : A–D, in fours (B 3 and 4 misplaced); 16 ff. ; 24 ll. Types 3, 4 and 5.

DESCRIPTION : [*Title*] This lytell Prac-‖tyce of Iohānes ‖ de Vigo in Medycyne/ is ‖ tranſlated out of Laten ‖ in to Englyſſhe/ for ‖ the helth of the ‖ body of man . ‖ [*Device No. 3*] (r.h.) Theſe medycynes were ‖ (l.h.) prouyed by Thorntone.

    Colophon : [Verso of D, 4] Imprynted by me Robert ‖ Wyer, dwellynge at the Sygne of ‖ Seynt Iohñ Euangelyſt, in ſeynt ‖ Martyns Pariſſhe, beſyde Cha-‖rynge Croſſe . ‖ Cum Priuilegio ad ‖ imprimendum solum.

COPY : British Museum (C. 31, a. 34).

REMARKS : This edition is page for page exactly as that with the "Suffolk" colophon, with slight variations in the spelling. The British Museum has another copy (7383, aaa.) of this edition, with the register correct.

98.— *Year Book, 9, Hen. IV.*   Folio.

REFERENCE: Herbert, Vol. 1, p. 377.

BOOKS PRINTED FOR SALE AT THE SIGN OF ST. JOHN THE EVANGELIST, AT CHARING CROSS.

ANDREWE, LAURENCE.   *Debate & Strife betwene Somer & Wynter.* n.d.   4to.

FAWKES, RICHARD.   *De Cursione Lune.*   n.d.   8vo.

PYNSON, RICHARD.   *Solomon & Marcolphus.*   n.d.   4to.

INDEX OF AUTHORS AND TITLES.

If you intende to please god / & wolde obteyne grace to fulfyll the same / two thynges ben vn to you very necessarye. The fyrste. you must withdrawe your mynde from all worldly and transytory thynges / in suche maner / as though you cared not whether any such thyn ges were in this worlde or no. The seconde is that you gyue and apply your selfe so wholy to god / and haue your selfe in suche a wayte / that you neuer do / saye / ne thynke / that you knowe suppose / or byleue shuld offede or dys please god / for by this meane / you may sonest and most redely obtayne / and wynne his fa uour & grace. In all thynges esteme and acout your selfe most vyle / and most symple / & as very nought in respecte / and regarde of ver tue and thynke / suppose / and byleue that all persons ben good / and better than you be / for so shall you moche please our lorde. What so euer you se / or seme to peryue / in any person / or yet here of any chrystyane / take you none oc casyon therin / but rather ascrybe / and applye you all vnto the best / and thynke or suppose / all is done or sayde for a good intent / or pur pose / though it seme cotrary. For mannes sus pycyons and lyght iudgementes ben soone / &

Type 1.
From *The Golden Pystle*, 1531.

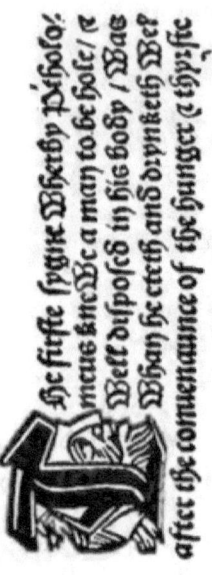

He fyrste fygure wherby philoso-
meus knewe y a man to be hole, &
well dysposed in his body / was
whan he eteth and drynketh well
after the contenaunce of the hunger & thyrste

Type 1 b.

From *The Compost of Ptholomeus*, c. 1532.

Yf men seme
to be punys-
shed for brea-
kynge of god
des lawe in
this world as
for cõmittige
aduoutry, for
nycacio, theft
heresy, and so
forth it is be-
cause the ma-
lyce of theyr
hertz breketh
forth, and dis-
qeieth theyr
neyghbours,
& therby offe-
deth y kyngs
lawe, & not i
that respecte
that they of-
fende goddes
lawe, whiche
is onely refer
red to god to
be punysshed
euerlastigly.

Type 2.

Side-note from *Defence of Peace*.

Prynted by me Robert wyer
foz wyllyam marfhall / and
fynyffhed in the moneth of
July in the yere of our
Lozde god a. M.
LLLLL.
xxxv.

And in the. xxbii. yere of the Reygne of our mofte
gracyous foueraygne lozde Henry the eyght,
by the grace of god, of Englande, and of
Fraunce kynge, defender of the
fayth, and lozde of Jrelande/
and fupzeme hed bnder
god of the churche
of Englande.

Types 3 and 5.
From *The Defence of Peace*, 1535.

AND oure Lozde,
wyl ɣ there ſhalbe
ſhewed .iiij. tokēs
after doctours ſa=
ynge, Foz our lozde is ſo mer=
cyfull that he wyl not punyſ=
ſhe vs but he wyl ſhewe ſome
tokens afoze. And ɣ we maye
be ſozy of our ſynnes, and do
penaſice. And after theſe foze=
ſayde. iiij. tokens ſhall yet be
xb. other tokens be ſhewed.
Which Jheronimus had foū=
den in the rinſkens Cronicle
of the Jewes. Of whiche.
xb. tokens fozeſayde ſhall be
declared by ozder here after.
℄ And the fyzſte token of the
iiij. ſhalbe that the myght of
A.ij.   Sathan

Type 4.
From *The iiii Tokens.*

¶ Erasmus to the good & god:
ly reader, wyssheth helthe in
our lorde Iesu chryste.

Remembre good
reader, that at an
other tyme also in
a certayn place, I
haue testifyed and
knowleged my selfe, to be verye
farre dysagreynge in oppynyon,
from those/ whiche do thynke ȳ
laye men & suche as be not learned ought vtterly to be kept far
awaye from the readynge of the
holy bokes and scryptures, to ȳ
which(as in the olde tyme, none
but the preestes entred, vnto the
most holy and moste secrete places of ȳ teple) they thynke none
shuld be admytted: or suffered to
haue

Type 5.

From Erasmus's *Exhortation to the Study of the Scriptures.*

CRobert Copland the tranſlatour herof to the Reders.

Entryll reders in conſydera=
cion that euery ſcyence, arte, and faculte that are
ſpeculate ᷓ pꝛactyſed by Phyloſophers, nat one=
ly ought to be ſhewed and taughte vnto ſuche as
be preſent with them in theyr dayes, but alſo foꝛ
a ſprctuall benefyte to be ſet foꝛth by wꝛytynges
vulgarily in euery tongue, foꝛ the moꝛe credines
and erudycyon of all yonge and pꝛegnaunt pꝛactyeyns, as ſayne
wolde attayne to the perfytenes of euery ſuche ſcyence, arte, and fa
culte. And nat withſtandynge that there be ryght many and ſondꝛy
coꝛies, aſwell of very good and ſcyentyke bokes, as of ryght expert
men within this Realme in the ſcyentycall arte of Cyꝛurgery. Ne=
uertheles this lytell queſtyonary ᷓ foꝛmulary with the other bokes
added therto haue ben often requyꝛed and ſoughte foꝛ, to be had in
engliſſhe (aſwell of me as of other, by dyuers and many perſones of
the ſayde ſcyence. In conſyderacyon aſoꝛeſayd, and that it is cōmo=
dyous, vtyle, behouefull, and benefycyall to the cōmon welth of the
ſayde ſcyence and arte. A certayne yonge gentyll man enured in the
ſayd ſcyence haue a boke of the ſame in frenche moued the ryght ho
neſt pſone Henry Dabbe bybliopolyſt ᷓ ſtacyoner to haue it tranſla
ted in to engliſſhe. At whoſe inſtigacyon meanynge the help of God
(though moſte rudely) with the ſymplenes of a good wyllyng herte
A haue enterpꝛyſed to do it in folowynge dyꝛectly my copy. Foꝛ A
knowlege myne enernyte in pꝛonouͤcyng the engliſſhe of the names
and termes naturally expꝛeſſed in the ſayde boke, aſwel in greke, la=
tyne, ᷓ other, whiche myne aucthour hath nat reduced in to frenche,
which names and termes A cōmpt to the dyſcrecyon, emendacyon,
and graunte of them that haue the perfytenneſſe of the ſayde ſcyence
and faculcie. Foꝛ as Phylyatros ſayeth, many termes and names
that are ſymply ſpoken in one language and ſcyence ſo harde to be
ſpoken in an other, except they be expꝛeſſed, and what they ſignyfye,
wherfoꝛe curteys and gentyll reders take this in woꝛth, and deſyꝛ
myne ygnoꝛaunce: in the ſame with your ſcyentycall beneuolence,
and clere frongſate intellygence. And Jeſus pꝛeſerue you. Amen.

CHereafter foloweth the queſtyo=
nary of Cyꝛurgyens.
CThe

Sarde and Garnat/ and Almandines / and Jargonce be all con=cerned togyther/but Jar=gonce hath the vertue of these stones / and it is the most fynest / and it gyveth a gentell red colour/and maketh a man mery and glad/ and kepeth hym longe yonge/and in great trouth/and maketh a man to forget his cō trarye. And also it staūcheth blode/and he that beryth it vpon hym / nedeth nat to drede to touche no euyll vermyn. And also he may passe all parellous places sewrely without daunger/and in what place that he cometh to / to be lodged in / he shall be gladly receyued & haue good chere / And any thyng that he asketh that is of reason shall nat be denyed hym/nor warned hym.

¶ The Topace. Cap. ij.

¶ Topace is of a yelowe colour/& there be of dyuers maners of Oryent/& of Arabye/ there

A.ij.

Types 7 and 5.
From the *Boke of the XXIIII Stones*.

MACERS HERBAL· PRACTY SYD BY DOCTOR· LYNACRO·

Tranſlated out of laten,
in to Englyſſhe, whiche
ſhewynge theyr Ope-
racyons & Uertues,
ſet in the margent
of this Boke, to
the entent you
myght knowe
theyr Uer-
tues.

Types 8 and 4.
From Macer's *Herbal*.

Device 1.
From the *Compost of Ptholomeus*, c. 1532.
[A very poor reproduction owing to bad state of original.]

Device 2.

From the *Golden Pystle* of St. Bernard, 1531.

Device 3.
From the *Golden Pystle* of St. Bernard, 1531.

www.ingramcontent.com/pod-product-compliance
Lightning Source LLC
Chambersburg PA
CBHW030006030726

47499CB00008B/2926